OT
CAMP
MURDER

a 'WE SIT PETS' mystery

MATTHEW ROSS

To Surjit
with best wishes

CURLEW CRESCENT

Cover Design by Patrick Knowles

ISBN: 9781739396398

ALSO BY **MATTHEW ROSS**

The 'Poynter & Perry' Tales

Death Of A Painter
The Red Admiral's Secret

The 'We Sit Pets' Mysteries

The Boot Camp Murder

Standalone (published by Burning Chair)

Burning Bridges

PRAISE FOR
DEATH OF A PAINTER

"A chaotic comic caper that's as funny as it is brutal"
– ***The Sun***, *national newspaper*

"With a cast of colourful characters and a riveting plot, Ross breathes new life into a classic genre."
– ***Julie Wassmer***, *author of The Whitstable Pearl series of mysteries, now a hit tv show produced by Acorn TV*

"I was humbled, honoured and above all else flabbergasted (in the nicest possible way) to be asked to provide an author quote for *Death Of A Painter* but it's easy when you're reading something as **funny, dark and touching** as this. Enjoy!"

- ***Jonathan Whitelaw***, *bestselling author of The Bingo Hall Detectives*

"A **rip-roaring blackly comic crime caper** that had me turning the pages extra-sharpish"

- ***Rob Parker***, *author of the Audible bestseller Far From The Tree*

"The story has everything – **excitement, edge of your seat action and a lot of humour**. It is fantastically well written, definitely a 'just one more chapter' type of book... It is **darkly comic and thrilling to the last page**... *Death of a Painter* is a fantastic read from an author who is going places."

- ***Chris McDonald***, *author of the D.I. Erika Piper mysteries*

"Do yourselves a favour and buy this book!"

– ***Evan Baldock***, *author of Bang, Bang, You're Dead!*

"**Five Stars**. Dark humour, quirky characters, murder, intrigue, a hint of romance, a gritty twist, and a narrative voice that is as entertaining as it is compelling. Everything, in fact, for an enjoyable crime romp."

– ***Frank Malley***, *author of The Lexford Town mysteries*

"If you like DIY, murder and cracking banter – this is the book for you!"

– ***Hazel Butterfield***, *broadcaster and author*

For Rebecca

CHAPTER **ONE**

9:30 A.M.: HE'D BEEN GOING ON FOR ALMOST AN HOUR. Most people by now would've rammed a pencil up the ignoramus's nose. Monica Minton instead gave a polite tight-lipped smile and acted professionally.

10:00 a.m.: Martin the Ignoramus had moved on to ranting furiously into his phone at some poor underling. Most people by now would've told him to calm down, take it easy. Monica Minton instead focused on her work in hand and acted professionally.

10:30 a.m.: Martin the Ignoramus loved an audience. In a packed and very public room he took great delight in berating Monica with such force and savagery his face turned red and his eyes bulged. Words like *pathetic, useless* and *incompetent* were hurled at her with contempt. Forming in the corners of his mouth, specks of white foam flew at her like a hail of bullets when he spat out phrases such as '*I should never have got a soppy bimbo to do a man's job, you're only here for decoration*' and '*if you spent less time gossiping with the rest of the airheads you might actually get something right for once.*' The reason for Martin the Ignoramus's outburst was to cover up the fact she'd followed his instructions to the letter; instructions based on his own abject failure to understand the task asked of him by the board. He'd shown the results to the senior team, always happy to take the credit for work he didn't do: ***I*** attach ***my*** report, I hope you like it. The senior team didn't like the report: ***his*** report. Most people by now would've been fighting back. Monica Minton instead remembered her mindfulness techniques, looked inward for her happy place and acted professionally.

10:33 a.m.: Monica Minton finally caught up with most people, albeit two hours and eight years too late.

'Can I just say ...' she repeated in a calm, level voice for the third time when Martin the Ignoramus finally paused for breath, 'Can I just say one thing ... I quit!'

Martin the Ignoramus's mouth hung open and his eyes bulged again, giving him the look of a stunned heifer. He struggled to comprehend what was happening. No-one had ever answered back before. This was the City of London, this was a safe space where pale stale males could bully, bray and bluster. He stared at the small young woman; she should be cowering, she should be respectful of his privilege and position. Nope, this did not compute: Martin floundered in stupefied silence.

'Workplace bullying,' Monica told the bewildered ignoramus. Realising all eyes were on her, she added, 'And everyone witnessed it.' Suddenly all eyes weren't on her anymore, and instead stared intensely at shiny shoes and VDUs. 'Constructive dismissal. You'll be hearing from my solicitor.'

Monica stood at her desk, unzipped her capacious handbag and gathered up her personal belongings; not much, given her long and loyal service, just a hairbrush, hand cream, a small selection of cosmetics and toiletries, a pen given to her by her father, half a box of earl grey teabags and a mug she received from Secret Santa that she wouldn't ordinarily ever give shelf-space to in her home, but, well, it was hers and she was taking it anyway. An out-of-date muesli bar and a blackened banana were dropped in the bin. Unpinning a couple of photos she'd had for decoration, she paused. Her hand hovered above her final item: a gift from her grandmother. Deciding she'd indulged the old woman's romantic fantastical whims long enough, she grabbed it, 'Fat lot of good you did', she said to the sprig of lucky heather. It joined the banana and bar in the bin. She was done.

Monica pulled on her jacket, and headed to the elevator. Where she'd expected to be carried along with a triumphant cheer from the downtrodden masses she instead heard her own heartbeat thumping loudly over the deathly silence. At least the eyes were back on her; she felt them hanging heavily on her shoulders as she waited for what seemed the slowest-moving elevator in the history of the world. It took forever to reach her on the ninth floor.

So slow: nope I'm not going to look back, hurry up lift, come on, hurry up. Eventually the doors slid open, 'You took your time getting here,' she said to the empty compartment. 'What did you do, come by post?'

In the rapid descent through nine storeys Monica plunged through nine different emotions. The doors opened on the busy ground floor reception with a ping; nobody expected the blubbering, quivering, hysterical wreck that tumbled out in a heap: 'Oh my god! What have I done?'

The snooty receptionist, behind her island of sleek white marble, looked over with disdain at the embarrassing sobbing mess sprawled across her lobby, unimpressed with the scene being created. Monica got up off her knees and wiped her eyes; trails of mascara dragged across her cheeks. She wailed again, and the snooty receptionist signalled to a nearby security guard: just the slightest of sideways glances, but he knew exactly what it meant.

Monica saw the guard in his thick black pullover and shiny polyester trousers heading towards her. Mistakenly thinking he was heading for the elevator, she stepped to her left. The guard, seeing the wailing woman hop out of his path, mistakenly thought she was attempting to avoid him and grabbed her elbow.

'You can't do this,' Monica shouted at the guard and 'He can't do this,' to anyone that might be watching, which of course was everybody although they all took great effort to pretend they weren't.

She struggled in the guard's grip. 'You do know you're not a real policeman, don't you? Just because you've got a hi-viz and a laminated badge doesn't mean you're a cop. Get off me!'

The guard released her into the open segment of an impressive revolving door – very shiny, very steel, very glass, very corporate – and gave it a shove. The heavy blade of the door swept up behind her and nudged her out on to the pavement. The realisation, like the first drops of rain, hit her square in the face.

'What've I done? What am I going to do?'

THE TRAIN HOME felt unnaturally empty. With an entire carriage to choose from, Monica picked her way around the seats before settling on one beside the window, her back to the direction of travel. A moment later she hopped to the one opposite, facing forwards: 'No looking back, look to the future, Monica,' she muttered. Taking a deep breath she turned her focus inward, seeking her happy place: it was closed and locked up for the day.

Sighing, she glanced around the carriage, wondering if this was the first time in the eight years she'd worked there she'd ever got a seat on the train. Her commutes to and fro were usually rush hour peak: trains packed to bursting, doors straining against the bodies crammed inside, elbows in her face, held fast like a fly caught in the tar-pit of humanity. Forced to listen to the escaping hiss from other people's headphones and forced to suffer in the miasma of other people's farts.

The train trundled slowly above familiar streets. An unpleasant sensation of nausea surged through her stomach when she realised what lay just around the bend. It lumbered past: fourteen storeys in curved green glass and steel, a modern monument to commerce and money in the bloody beating heart of London. Monica's home-from-home since joining the graduate scheme: IGR Financial, a world leading financial consultancy, and the company made certain the staff knew how lucky they were to be a part of it. *Only the best are good enough for IGR*, so said the mantra; *if you can't cut it you aren't good enough*, implied the unspoken follow-up. Anyone leaving was deemed a failure, their existence airbrushed from history. Maybe it motivated some but maybe it demoralised just as many, if not more.

In the few seconds it took to pass IGR, Monica's head swum with a million thoughts: *What am I going to do, will I still get paid, how much money have I got in the bank, what about my savings, will I get another job, what do I say when asked why I left my job, who'll give me a reference, what if I can't find another job ... WHAT DO I TELL MY MOTHER?*

Monica took a long deep breath, closed her eyes and looked inward for her happy place only to find it boarded up, burnt out and smouldering.

THE JOGGER HAD RUN the same circuit in recent days; always the same route, always the same time. Nearing completion of her first lap, she spotted him walking towards her. As she approached, he caught her eye and smiled. Her face warmed beyond the pink flush of exercise; the delicious thrill of being noticed. Coyly she tucked a strand of hair behind her ear and jogged on, already planning on how to play it cool on her second time round, whilst rehearsing what she'd say on her third and final pass, convinced today was the day she'd summon up the confidence to introduce herself.

Paddy, aware of the effect he'd had on the jogger, chuckled to himself: *yep, still got it,* whatever *it* may be, but there was no time for celebrations because around his feet four dogs jostled for his attention; dogs of differing size but of equal energy and exuberance. Paddy dropped to a knee, threw wide his arms: 'Group hug!' Sharing the excitement of four happy dogs clambering all over him it was hard to tell who was the soppiest and dopiest of the bundle, although Paddy probably just about edged it.

'Come on guys,' he rose back up, 'let's go.'

The dogs bounced with unbridled joy, winding their leashes together in a happy furry maypole. If the jogger had seen his grin at the sight of his dogs' glee it would've made her weaker at the knees than her daily 5K. Paddy gave the dogs the pats and strokes they so desperately sought and untangled their leashes. With a click of the tongue and a flick of the wrist he got them all walking ahead of him. No pulling or aggression or veering off; they prowled proudly, they were a pack, Paddy was their alpha dog and they loved their leader.

The sun hung low. The ground was soft. The overnight rainstorm had left everything with a clean, refreshed look this morning. The grass was a deep verdant green, the crocuses and snowdrops were beginning to bud and the air was heavy with that reassuring loamy smell of springtime. Paddy loved days like this. He was reflecting on how much he loved being out with the dogs and how much he loved his life when he felt a tug to his left. He glanced down, one of the leashes had become taut: a grey Staffie had taken itself away from the group. It squatted and its muscular back rippled with the force of contraction. Paddy's thoughts of self-congratulation evaporated: 'Oh, Roxy! Do you have to?'

THE RIVERSIDE PARK began as a few hectares of scrubland, saved by conversationists as a refuge for birds and wildlife back when developers started demolishing the old warehouses to build waterside apartments about fifteen years ago. It immediately became a popular retreat for families, walkers, joggers and birdwatchers – so much so the council built them a visitors' centre and café on the edge of the car park; a large rustic timber barn, sensitively repurposed for its new life. This morning a school party lined up outside: forty or so unruly kids in what vaguely resembled single file, marshalled by two exhausted-looking women in hi-viz waistcoats desperately trying and failing to do a headcount of the writhing mass.

Monica avoided the melee of children and scanned the wide, flat expanse for her brother, Paddy. He wasn't at home when she'd got back; his text said he'd be getting to the park around ten and would be there for around an hour and a half. She checked her watch: *eleven thirty-five, he can't be far away, he must be on his way back by now.* She headed down from the car park towards the start of the path, pulling on her gloves. She remembered her sunglasses in her pocket, thought for a second then put them on: *I don't want him knowing I cried all the way home.*

HEARING A WOMAN call his name in public triggered mixed emotions for Paddy: it could go fifty-fifty, either good times lie ahead, or trouble had arrived. From the tone of voice, he couldn't tell which. He turned slowly, unsure what to expect. He felt relieved but oddly disappointed to find it was his sister, wearing a look of bewilderment.

'Oh, Monica, it's only you, here, catch.' He tossed her a small black plastic bag knotted at the top.

Acting on reflex Monica trapped it between her two palms. It was only when the soft warm parcel squished within her grip that she realised what she was holding. Her next reflex action: she flung it as far as she could. 'Eeugh! Paddy!'

'What? You're wearing gloves,' Paddy managed to say, gulping down breaths between laughing, 'Come on, we'll have to go and get that back, otherwise I'll get fined if I leave it.'

'Eeugh! No. Who's going to fine you? The Poop Police?'

'Look ... over there.'

Monica followed Paddy's finger to a small figure in the distance: a muscly man in extremely close-fitting scarlet Lycra shorts and a top so tight it could have been painted on. She nodded.

'See him? Looks like a superhero on his day off? That's my arch-enemy.'

'Your what?'

'My arch-enemy.' Paddy's voice carried a serious tone, adding a harsh explosion to the 'ch' sound. 'Boot Camp Dan. Personal trainer. Gets them running and jumping and all sorts. He actually accused me of stealing his equipment. See those plastic cones and kettlebell weights? Claimed I'd stolen some, to try and get me barred from the park.' Paddy's eyes never left the distant figure. Even this far away Monica knew the figure was staring back too, both of them locked in seething eye contact. 'And if he finds any poo on the ground, he blames me ... well, he blames the dogs, but you know what I mean.'

'Let's go get it then,' replied Monica, not keen to handle the package again but desperate to break up the long-range staring contest that she'd started to find quite awkward. 'And that's what I was going to ask ... whose are these dogs?'

Paddy looked down around his feet, as though seeing them for the first time, and then using his chin to point said, 'That's Beyoncé, that's Bruno, that one's Roxy and that's Winkle.'

'Not *who* are the dogs, Paddy, *whose* are the dogs?'

That particular penny had a long way to go before it finally dropped and then, as if by magic, a glimmer of understanding shone in Paddy's eyes, 'Oh, I walk them. That's what I do now, walk dogs ... between gigs.'

Monica knew she'd regret it but couldn't help herself. 'Gigs?'

'My DJ sets.' A hurt tone implied she'd offended him by not remembering his one true vocational calling but, never the best at spotting social cues, Monica persisted:

'DJ-ing is it now? What happened to the rock band?'

'We split for musical differences.'

'And the theatre group?'

'We're on hiatus, after Mike got a job at Aldi.'

'And the novel?'

'Writer's block.'

'So now you're walking dogs?'

'It's only temporary, just until my big break.' Paddy had such certain belief: *in twelve months' time I'll be famous.* The only trouble was he'd thought that twelve months ago, and twelve months before that, and twelve months before that and, well, way back to when he was still at school.

The glossy dark hair and deep blue, almost violet, eyes marked Paddy and Monica out as siblings. Romantic and fanciful family legend claimed their colouring was a throwback to a possible Huguenot ancestry, but in truth it was more than likely thanks to the afternoon their Victorian great-great-great-grandmother enjoyed below-stairs with a gypsy coalman that led to her dismissal as scullery maid. Hair and eyes aside, that was as far as any family resemblance went. Where Monica was driven, Paddy was laid-back, where Monica was scholarly, Paddy was laid-back, where Monica had a five-year career plan, Paddy was laid-back.

Paddy had coasted through life so far with very few obstacles, getting by on good looks, blissful ignorance and a cheerful demeanour. Very much their mother's golden child, everything had come easily to Paddy, and as far as he knew that's how the world worked.

'People pay you to walk their dog?'

'Yep! They might be sick, or on holiday. Or they might not be home as they're working sixty hours a week, which ...' Paddy threw her a quizzical look, 'begs the question, what are you doing here? On a Tuesday. Are you allowed to be out in the wild on a work day?'

In yet another way the siblings differed, Paddy's ability to understand and empathise with people was miles above anything his sister possessed; when his simple question hung in the air unanswered, he immediately spotted her eyes moisten a little.

'Ah, it's like that, is it? Monica, walk this way.'

PADDY LED HER to a dilapidated mobile cabin on the edge of the park, close to the river: 'It's nothing fancy,' he said modestly, but modesty wasn't required. No humblebrag here. It really was nothing fancy, in fact fancy was probably busy looking up the libel laws feeling seriously aggrieved it'd even been in the same sentence.

Paddy wafted his arm in an extravagant gesture. '*Et voilà*, welcome to the Munsters'.'

Just as Monica asked, 'Why'd you call it the Munsters'?', a small squat man with a bald sphere of a head and an ear that looked as though the dog had enjoyed a good chew on it appeared at the serving hatch. He was missing alternate teeth and had a heavy monobrow that made him look very stern. 'Never mind,' she added.

Monica looked the cabin up and down, as though trying to spot patterns in the swirling green algae that covered it. 'Can't we go to the visitor centre instead? That looked nice. And it's indoors,' she added, eyeing the wet, greying plastic patio set with disdain.

'No way,' snapped Paddy, 'Boot Camp Dan's got it stitched up in some deal with the manager, he lets him get changed in there. Besides, I like it here. It's got character.'

'It's got cholera, more like.' Monica compared the seats, looking for the one with the least amount of seagull splatter. Success. She found the clean one, well relatively, and clutched the leashes pressed into her hand by Paddy.

Paddy waited beside the serving hatch, trying and failing to elicit any conversation with the sallow-faced man inside, until: 'Thanks, mate.' Paddy took two takeaway cups from him and brought them over. 'So, what are you going to tell Mum?'

Monica winced. 'I was actually kind of hoping you'd tell her for me,' she said, praying Paddy would show some sibling solidarity in her moment of need but instead of listening Paddy was prising the flimsy plastic lid from the cup he held. He took a suspicious sip. 'Yuk, tastes flowery, must be yours.' He passed the Earl Grey tea across.

'Thanks.' She took the cup from him and brought it in close to her with both hands, feeling its warmth against her chest. 'So, will you tell Mum for me?'

Paddy's eyes opened wide across the rim of his cup. He coughed down the mouthful he'd just swigged and spluttered, 'Me? Why me?'

'Because you're her little treasure. You know you are. If I tell her I've quit my job I'd never hear the end of it, she'd never let me forget it. But you, her Golden Baby Boy, you could tell her anything. You could be indicted for war crimes in the Hague and it wouldn't faze her, in fact she'd be so proud of her handsome little prince getting his name in the newspapers she'd be telling all the neighbours.'

'That's unfair,' Paddy protested, despite knowing it was true, and secretly liking the handsome bit.

Beneath her seat Monica felt movement: a cold wet nose pressed against her bare ankle, causing her to shriek. Paddy gave a half-smile of the kind that had melted a hundred women near and far.

'How about if I let you off this month's rent? Will you tell her for me?' suggested Monica. It sounded a grand offer but both knew it meaningless, given Paddy hadn't paid any rent since moving in with her two years earlier and probably never would, but at least it'd save him the effort of concocting some elaborate reason why not this month.

'Okay, I'll talk with her tonight.'

Monica thanked him profusely, and watched fondly as he tousled the jowls of a soppy-looking Labrador lying at his feet.

'So, what are you going to do for money?' he asked, looking into the eyes of the dog, but Monica suspected the question was for her.

'I've no idea. I've not thought that far. I'll sign up with a few agencies, go on a few websites, and hopefully find something suitable,' she said, thinking aloud, and convincing neither of them.

'That could take weeks.' Paddy spoke with an authority that belied the fact he'd never ever actually held a proper job in his life. 'What are you going to do in the meantime?'

'I've got some savings ...' mumbled Monica but her voice trailed away, demonstrating she had about as much belief as she did collateral.

'You can help me if you like,' offered Paddy. 'I'm getting calls all the time; people wanting their dogs walked and their cats fed. There's just not enough hours in the day, I turn most of them down.'

'Walking dogs? Feeding cats?' Monica could tell from the embarrassment blooming on Paddy's face that she must have added too much scorn to her voice and tried to backtrack, 'It's just that ... I don't think so ... my background ... business and finance, not ... this.' She raised a limp hand to gesture at nothing in particular.

'Just thought you could've done with the cash.' Paddy's reply made no attempt to mask the passive-aggressive *up yours* he was giving her. 'I didn't want anything out of it, whatever they paid would've been all yours. Probably a couple of hundred a day for three hours' work. But you're not interested, fine, I can always ask—'

'Wait. Two hundred pounds? For three hours' work?'

'If that. Collect four dogs, walk them for an hour, take them home, collect four more, walk them for an hour too, take them home. Rest of the day's yours.'

'And there's a big enough market for this?'

'Honestly, I'm getting calls every day—'

If Paddy was still talking Monica didn't notice, she'd tuned out. Her first thought, *If there's that much money in it, pay me some rent,* was quickly set aside. An idea had sprouted inside her: *My business brains, his ... well ... him ... working together we sit pets, this could be a winner!*

On the horizon Boot Camp Dan chivvied an overweight middle-aged woman into doing star jumps. With every melancholy beat of the jumping woman's bingo-wings Monica's idea took shape.

'Put it there, partner.' She thrust her hand at Paddy. Instead of a handshake she got a face of confusion. 'In business together, you and me – *We Sit Pets.*'

CHAPTER **TWO**

ALL THE GEAR AND NO IDEA. Nine o'clock sharp, a fully prepared Monica met Paddy for her first day in the field.

'Who've you come as? Princess Anne?'

As well as spending all night drafting business plans and forecasts with brightly coloured graphs and whizzy pie charts, Monica had been shopping. Clad head to foot in brand-new outdoors equipment, Monica stood ready for her new venture, dressed for success: waterproof waxed jacket, thermal layers, sun hat, knee-high welly boots- the full kit, and most of the kaboodle too. Everything was fresh out of the box and on today. She was ready, confident and prepared for anything.

'Got poo bags?' asked Paddy.

Poo bags, I forgot the poo bags, of all the things to forget. Monica shook her head.

'Here you go, then,' replied Paddy tossing something her way. Feeling the soft warm squelch between her fingers she realised she'd fallen for the same prank as before. *I wonder if I'll live to regret this,* she wondered to herself.

MONICA AND PADDY WALKED together; Paddy had arranged with his fellow dog-walking friends to meet later on at the Munsters'. The path ahead was obscured by a long sweeping curve following the contours of the riverbank. As they rounded it, they were almost knocked off their feet by an angry little blur appearing with urgent surprise from the hedgerow. A furious little man fumed before them. Dressed top to toe in his camouflage-wear, rage bubbled beneath the ginger crewcut. Without even a cursory excuse me the man vented his anger: 'Have you seen what he's done?'

'Pete ... mate ... what's wrong?' asked Paddy.

Pete, for that was his name, gestured wildly in no particular direction. His arm turned quicker than a windmill on a spin cycle: the frenzied activity diverted any power of thought, he couldn't speak through his fury, so Paddy filled the silence.

'Monica, this is Pete. He's the president of the birdwatching group down here—'

'The peninsula!' Pete had found his voice. 'It was the best nesting site for waterbirds in the South East. We respected it, and because of that the birds respected us—'

Paddy and Monica shared a sideways glance that suggested they didn't understand Pete's comment but knew it didn't sound right.

'But what he's done, it's ... eco-vandalism, that's what it is. This time of year, it's when the moorhens and the red kites nest. They won't with that circus going on, all that commotion'll scare 'em off this year. Maybe forever. It's not right. I won't let it lie.' Pete dragged the back of his hand across his nose with a long snort, then stomped off.

'What a peculiar man,' commented Monica after a moment or two's pause for reflection. Paddy shrugged a non-committal response and they resumed their walk.

It didn't take long to round the curve in the riverbank, and a sight awaited them they weren't expecting but it was clearly what had got Pete so vexed. On the flat peninsula that jutted out into the river, a small but impressive-looking stage had been erected. Glittery streamers fluttered in the breeze. *"Boot Camp Dan"* read the banners vertically either side of the stage in neon yellow. A backdrop curtain hung behind the stage, also emblazoned with the *"Boot Camp Dan"* brand name in the same vivid lettering. A short distance in front of the stage stood a stubby, small scaffold tower: its platform topped out around eight feet off the ground. A pair of powerful spotlights more at home in a theatre hung off the front; by remote control they swivelled from side to side like machine guns in a turret. At ground level, an earnest looking young man took his duties very seriously, prowling the area with a professional-looking TV camera perched on his shoulder and his eyeball pressed tightly against the viewfinder. Between the tower and the stage, twenty-four collapsible chairs had been erected and arranged in three rows – all that was missing were the bums on seats.

Next to the stage three eager young people stood around with headsets, clipboards and walkie-talkies hanging from their belts. They looked with rapt attention at a handsome smoothie in a striped blazer giving them last-minute instructions.

Noticing a flicker of movement on the periphery of his vision Smoothie looked across, towards Paddy and Monica. He raised a finger, the universal sign language for 'wait, just a moment' to the young tech crew and approached Monica and Paddy in a stride that was too fast for a walk, too slow for a run but loaded with purpose: 'You can't be here!' his voice ingrained with that sort of authority a good public school provides, 'We're going live in less than twenty minutes.'

'Is that right?' Paddy dipped his forehead towards the stage. 'I thought this was a public park?'

Smoothie gave a polite, nervous laugh, unsure whether Paddy was serious.

Paddy was.

Monica, sensing the tension between the two men, felt compelled to play the diplomat. 'It looks very fancy.'

The Smoothie noticed the small woman behind Paddy for the first time; peculiar, in the way she dressed, it reminded him of his great-aunt: a formidable woman who terrorised the Scottish Highlands hunting, shooting, fishing anything that moved. He instantly felt self-conscious and the need for best manners, just in case she too concealed a double-barrelled shotgun somewhere about her person. 'Thank you. We'll be broadcasting at exactly ten o'clock, so that's in ...' he tilted his wrist, 'eighteen minutes. I've spent weeks planning this live launch, I can't afford anything to go wrong, the investors will be here any minute.' Looking over and beyond her shoulder, he broke off from what he was about to say; gesticulating, he shouted to the young camera-operator nearby, 'Surjit, over there! I told you, we need more scenic background shots for the package.'

Surjit, the young man with the camera, showed his assent by turning his attention to capture panoramic images of the sunlight reflecting off the water.

'Sorry about that. He's only a student. They all are actually, they're all from the media studies course at the college,' he gestured towards the three eager assistants with the walkie talkies and clipboards, 'They're here for work experience. It's just you need to remind them every now and again this is the real world, not some college assignment.'

The small woman looked straight at him with such an intensity it brought forth memories of his Great-Aunt Isobel striding across the Cairngorms on yet another killing spree. It unnerved him, causing him to gabble: 'Sorry. Where were we? Oh yes, my name's James Doyle. I'm a business angel. I take small businesses, introduce them to the right investors and turn them into household brands. Right now, we're going to launch Boot Camp Dan as the new fitness brand. Your own personal trainer, available online, just click and subscribe, either follow along with the live class, or participate at a time that suits using our online archive.'

'Can't we stay and watch?' Monica's disappointment sounded genuine. 'I'm an entrepreneur too, you know.'

'No. I'm really sorry, I must ask you to move along,' he replied, his tone courteous yet economic. 'Let's talk later,' he offered out of politeness; a promise he had absolutely no intention of honouring, and he was gone, already barking orders at a young man with a clipboard.

'BOOT CAMP DAN, unleashed on the world. How can that man sleep at night?'

Mr Munster glowered from his serving hatch, but the people at the table laughed at Paddy's retelling of their encounter with James Doyle. They'd gathered for Paddy as promised, and after ordering teas from Mr Munster, Paddy quickly made the introductions.

'Right,' he pulled the flimsy lid from his cup and took a sip. 'Monica, this is everyone, yuk, flowery: must be yours,' he said through a lemony wince, swapping his tea with Monica. Paddy gestured at the nearest person, a cheerful middle-aged lady in a raspberry gilet with a white turtleneck under.

'I'm Hazel,' she chirruped. She wore a matching raspberry baker's boy cap perched at a jaunty angle over her smart silver bob. Her outfit was very retro Swinging Sixties, but she appeared the sort of woman who'd found a look that suited her and stuck with it rather than a follower of fashions. When she spoke she used a tone that suggested an old-fashioned education back when speaking correctly was still important. 'I'm a family archivist.'

'Oh, really,' replied Monica in that way that said *I have no idea what you're talking about but I'm being polite*. Hazel picked up on it and was glad to explain for Monica's benefit, leading Monica to wonder whether Hazel's favourite subject could very well be Hazel.

'I was a librarian for almost thirty years,' she began, 'until they closed the libraries. What can you do now Hazel, I said to myself, and then it came to me: all those years of research and archiving, you might as well put it to good use – so now I build people's family trees for them! Traced one chap's line right back to the Great Fire of London recently, amazing stuff. If you want yours done, let me know.'

'Err ... thanks,' replied Monica, unsure whether the offer was serious but knowing she didn't want every dirty little family secret exposed and laid bare by this total stranger.

Paddy, with a flick of his chin, pointed at a young man with a scruffy copse of beard, square-rimmed glasses and an old navy fleece jacket, pilled and bobbled through age.

'So, this here's Comedy Tim,' said Paddy. Tim looked up from his phone, mouthed hello, then looked down again. He wiggled his thumb, texting at lightning speed. 'Tim is a stand-up comic and writer. He's going to be a big star one day, aren't you?' Tim looked a bit bashful at Paddy's high praise. He muttered something no-one could hear; Monica wondered if public speaking was possibly not the right calling for this young man.

'That reminds me, Tim' continued Paddy, 'How was the audition?'

Monica spotted the wide eyes of faux pas on Hazel; Paddy didn't. 'Tim met with some industry bigwigs yesterday,' he explained to Monica, 'about writing and performing on a new radio comedy show. Might even make it to TV if it's popular, isn't that right, Tim? So, how did it go?'

Monica, pre-warned by Hazel's expression, had a fair idea how it went. Paddy clearly didn't as he looked expectantly to Tim for a response.

'And this here is Kenton,' Hazel offered to divert everyone's attention from Comedy Tim, and indicated a large man filling the last garden chair. He looked like he'd been carved out of ebony by a sculptor with blunt chisels and not enough time for the finer details: his hands were huge and angular like shovels, his shoulders were as wide and square as a gravestone, his head a solid oblong with a flat straight nose and a brow overhanging straight and level like an awning.

'Kenton's a boxing coach. He's got a couple of good young prospects, proper contenders,' added Paddy.

'Interesting,' replied Monica, 'So we've got a comedian, an archivist and a boxer, and ...' her voice tailed off as she reached Paddy, unsure how to finish her sentence.

'A superstar DJ,' responded Paddy, eagerly picking up her dropped train of thought.

'You've all got second jobs?' queried Monica.

'No,' replied Paddy. Monica didn't understand but couldn't miss the sound of someone chuckling at his answer.

'Those *are* our jobs,' explained Comedy Tim.

'Dog-walking's just what we do to earn extra cash, so we can pursue those jobs,' explained Archivist Hazel. Boxer Kenton didn't speak, just nodded his agreement.

Paddy looked around the table, then faced his sister: 'In fact, Monica, the only professional dogwalker here ... is you.'

FOR MOST PEOPLE faced with that revelation, a crisis of confidence would ensue. But not Monica. She felt inspiration surge; her commercial and management acumen flashed awake. Instantly, she sensed opportunity. Excited, she hurriedly shared her thoughts with the others. By the time she'd finished and seen their reactions, she knew she'd have been better off explaining it to the dogs instead.

'So ... what ... we work for you now?' asked Tim. He'd looked up from his phone to glance around the table for reassurance; getting none, his attention fell back to his phone.

'Not exactly,' replied Monica.

'What does that mean? Either we do or we don't,' insisted Hazel. Kenton gave an impatient grunt of support.

'What I'm suggesting,' explained Monica, 'is that my company, *We Sit Pets*, becomes your agency. I'll handle the marketing and the clients, and all the boring admin.' She'd added invisible quotes finger gestures to the last two words, hoping it'd persuade them they'd be better off leaving it all to her. She noticed the sideways glances shuttling around the table and realised she may have misjudged her audience. She persisted, 'I'll handle all the day-to-day business stuff, all you have to do is walk the dogs, feed the cats and wash the goldfish. Your payment's guaranteed at the end of the week.'

Hazel didn't sound convinced. 'But I already walk dogs and I get paid. No problem.'

'Well—' Monica began, desperately trying to think of something to say.

'Sick,' interrupted Paddy, 'What if you're sick?'

'Yes, exactly, sick,' she said, grasping the conversational baton offered by Paddy. She gave a small nod in Paddy's direction, just the smallest of gestures, barely noticeable but he recognised her gratitude for coming to her rescue. 'What happens when you feel like you're at death's door with a nasty virus? Would you still go out?'

'Of course not,' replied Hazel.

'And what about the dogs? What happens if it's one of those bugs that lasts a week, or longer? What would the owners do? Find someone else?'

Hazel sought a response: her mouth opened and flapped but no words came. She bobbed her head and raised her palms to concede the point.

'If you come with me, any time you're sick or want a holiday, I'd be able to call on someone else from my list to cover. The dogs get walked, the clients are happy, everything carries on fine.'

'That's a good point,' Tim said, addressing the others. 'I only got these dogs because the girl that used to do them went to the Caribbean—'

'Jamaica?' said Paddy, cueing up Comedy Tim for the perfect punchline.

'Antigua, I think. Why?'

'Never mind.'

Paddy gave the faintest shake of the head in exasperation towards Monica, who again wondered whether Tim was cut out to be a comedian, not that he'd noticed their disappointment in his lack of funny bones as he pressed on. 'I'll give it a go, why not?'

'Okay, me too,' added Hazel, 'But you promise I'll still get paid, no problems, no cheats.'

Monica confirmed again she would guarantee their payments, and then turned to face Kenton. 'How about you? Are you in?'

'I am,' replied Kenton. He spoke with a smooth, deep baritone in a calm and measured voice, 'on one condition.'

'Okay, what's that?'

'If you're serious about looking after us,' Kenton twisted in his chair and swung a heavy muscular arm for emphasis, 'get Boot Camp Dan off our backs.'

'Yes! He's nothing but a nuisance and a bully,' agreed Hazel.

'Boot Camp Dan,' muttered Tim with an acid tone. 'Can't stand him!'

'Did I tell you he accused me of stealing his stuff again last week?' Paddy added to the atmosphere of discontent.

Monica knew what she needed to do: 'Deal!'

Dropping the leash she'd been holding, she thrust her hand out expecting it to be shaken vigorously. It stayed there until it became awkward. With a jerk she brought it back and smoothed down her hair. 'Leave it with me! I'll make it happen.' Remembering the leash she'd been holding she looked around for it. 'Hold on, where's Winkle?'

In the distance a small black and tan projectile was approaching terminal velocity. Glad to be released from bondage the perky Border terrier had seen his chance for freedom and lunged at it. He was off at double quick speed, his little stumpy legs moved like a blur and had no intention of slowing down.

CHAPTER **THREE**

AT THE SAME MOMENT WINKLE THE BORDER TERRIER was vanishing over the horizon, Pamela in Aberdeenshire was logging in to her computer: *I mustn't be late, it'll be starting soon.*

Although located at the opposite end of the country, Pamela was very interested in what was happening at the Riverside Conservation Park – or rather, *who* was happening. Pamela was Boot Camp Dan's biggest fan.

'He's gorgeous,' she would coo to everyone in the bakery where she worked: only three mornings a week mind, ever since Mum had her funny turn last November. Luckily this was a "watch with mother" morning. They huddled around Pamela's old and clunky laptop. It was as thick and grey as a paving slab and about as quick to turn on.

Mother blew out an impatient sigh; she was missing *Homes Under the Hammer* for this, but Pamela seemed insistent they watch it together and it wasn't worth the argument. 'You'll love it Mum, he's such a hunk. Wait 'til you see his muscles, and his smile, he's got the cutest dimples. And he's funny, so funny. Let me read you some of today's tweets.' Mother groaned inwardly and endured Pamela, never a naturally gifted joke-teller, reciting half a dozen quips and puns read from her phone with the warmth and humour of a constipated parking meter.

Pamela was indeed Boot Camp Dan's biggest fan – but the competition was fierce. By some complicated, ingenious computer trickery an algorithm had been deployed to target Pamela and tens of thousands of women just like her all across the internet. It had been developed by that handsome smoothie, business angel James Doyle. Coupled with his strategic recruitment of top stylists and designers, so began the cult of Boot Camp Dan. James had thought of everything, there was even a ghostwriter to manage the social media, and provide the witty posts and funny quips so enjoyed by Pamela every day. For the past six months viewing figures had steadily grown as, three times a week, Boot Camp Dan's YouTube channel broadcast sessions live from the Riverside Conservation Park with edited highlights and bonus footage uploaded to the channel every other day; James's plan was working, they were aggressively hitting the market and now advertisers and investors were on the scent, sensing a killing was to be made.

Some fans joined in with Boot Camp Dan's exercise sessions; posting photos to his social media of themselves mirroring his exertions, to be rewarded with likes and thumbs-up emojis from the man himself – or so they thought; never once suspecting there was a ghostwriter under the strictest instructions that Boot Camp Dan, meaning *they,* will respond to every single message personally. Pamela however, like many others, preferred their Boot Camp Dan exercise sessions more sedentary, preferably with a nice cup of tea: *slice of cake, Mum?*

With moments to spare the ancient laptop woke up; it gave a noisy whir of its fans, and the screen blinked colourfully to life. A few impatient clicks took them to Boot Camp Dan's channel: 'Here we go Mum, you comfortable, more cake?'

Upbeat, high-tempo dance music and the big voiceover: "*Here's ... Boot Camp Dan!*" The show was starting. *Boot Camp Dan,* thought Pamela, *you look particularly fine today in your black and yellow outfit, mighty fine indeed.*

The music faded out. In Aberdeenshire, Pamela edged closer to her laptop in anticipation, Boot Camp Dan was about to speak, here it comes ...

Boot Camp Dan looked directly down the camera and into the eyes of the viewers at home; all across the internet women of a certain age were set a-flutter at the sight; in the park the invited audience of investors applauded politely. Boot Camp Dan opened his mouth, about to speak, but ... paused. He turned his head away, looking in a direction off to the distance. Something had distracted him. What could it be, they all wondered. And then coming louder and closer from off-camera they heard the plaintive wail: 'Winkle!'

MONICA DIDN'T REALISE she was being livestreamed to tens of thousands of confused ladies when she dashed back and forth across Boot Camp Dan's 'fitness zone'.

Monica chased and she lunged and she pounced and she fell and she sprinted and she stretched and at no point did she come even close to the Border terrier who tore across the landscape like a furry Exocet: 'Winkle!'

Boot Camp Dan sizzled in white-hot fury: *how dare she? How very dare she!* The smile had gone, replaced by the kind of scowl that'd curdle milk. His jaw tensed and the veins in his neck began to bulge. Boot Camp Dan was not happy, even Pamela in Aberdeenshire could see that.

Boot Camp Dan couldn't comprehend what was happening here, in his fitness zone, on his launch event: *what is going on, don't they know who I am?*

Winkle the Border terrier either didn't notice Boot Camp Dan's ire, or he didn't care. He was having far too much fun weaving slaloms around the lighting rigs he'd found. Plus, the strange lady chasing him made it even more fun.

'Winkle ... Winkle ... Winkle,' but Monica's shouts fell on deaf ears, heard by everyone apart from the intended. She was certainly moving at quite a pace. 'Is this usually what happens?' Mother asked the dumbfounded Pamela, just as Winkle exited screen-left pursued by a Monica. The sound of her repeated calling of his name receded into the distance. Boot Camp Dan remained motionless on the screen, watching them off-camera; a nasty snarl curled his lip until it almost touched his nose. Then, all at once, remembering the camera was rolling, he suddenly changed back into smiling, jovial Boot Camp Dan again. The cheeky chappie flashed his gleaming white teeth to the viewers at home.

'Well, that was certainly unexpected,' Boot Camp Dan said through a broad smile that didn't correspond with his cold eyes. 'That's live broadcasting for you. Anything can happen.' Boot Camp Dan's gaze flicked nervously to a direction off-camera. Reassuring himself that the disturbance was gone, he continued, 'Welcome, we've got a great session ahead, ideal for those bums and tums, get ready to work those glutes to the maximus—'

The problem for Boot Camp Dan was he'd looked in the wrong direction. Just as he set his feet shoulder-width apart to demonstrate his technique for the perfect squat something resembling a small hairy cannon ball shot through his legs at high velocity.

'What the—?' muttered Boot Camp Dan - over time, viewers would debate and disagree at length whether he was referring to the galloping animal between his feet or being clattered into from behind a split second later by a speeding Monica. In Aberdeenshire Pamela gasped her surprise, meanwhile Mother clapped and chuckled: this was turning out so much better than she'd expected, she hadn't minded missing *Homes Under the Hammer* in the slightest.

James Doyle reacted immediately, Surjit the camera operator however didn't. 'Cut, cut, stop filming, stop,' demanded James at the sight of his investment being face-planted to the floor. Surjit kept filming, convinced his payday had come at last. Boot Camp Dan hadn't paid him anything, not a penny, to cover all those mornings spent filming: *trust me, this is good exposure for you*, he'd said, *get this on your résumé and you'll get a job anywhere*, he'd said. It'd sounded convincing, but then the mornings filming began to include evenings editing, again all supposedly good experience: *this will definitely get you a job on* The One Show, *mark my words, you'll thank me later*. Sometimes it was as though Surjit was invisible when Boot Camp Dan and James spoke, maybe they thought he couldn't hear them: 'The YouTube channel is up three hundred percent on last month, the investors are loving it, it's an advertiser's dream.' Meanwhile, Surjit hadn't even been offered so much as a hot chocolate to warm him up after yet another cold and damp morning stuck outside. So, when Surjit saw the chaos unfurling before him, he knew he'd struck comedy gold: *the internet will love this, it'll go viral in minutes.*

BOOT CAMP DAN flapped away James's offered arm and stood up by himself, brushing off the dirt from his knees as he straightened. The bright yellow flashes of Lycra around his shoulders were smeared with grubby grey stains from where he'd bounced across the stage floor. Boot Camp Dan's eyes bulged and his teeth bared. He spun around to face his assailant: 'You!'

Monica gave a meek raise of her hand. 'Sorry. It was an accident. You see, I—'

'You,' repeated Boot Camp Dan, the fury rising in his tone. 'I should have guessed it would've been either the cretin or the cretin's sister.'

James made a peacekeeping intervention. 'Come on, that's a bit harsh.' His gallantry was noted by Monica: *such a gentleman.* 'She said it was an accident.'

'My dog got loose,' Monica explained, pointing at Winkle who by now had exhausted himself and besides, it was no fun now the silly lady wasn't playing anymore. He'd flopped at her feet, threw a hind leg over his shoulder and began licking himself intimately to pass the time.

Boot Camp Dan wasn't listening, he leaned in close to Monica going eyeball to eyeball. 'How dare you,' his finger jabbed at her, 'how dare you come into my space, on to my live launch show and ruin it. How dare you. Do you know who I am?'

As Monica paused to consider her response, the grey clouds above her parted and a shaft of sunlight penetrated through: a coincidence or a sign? Monica didn't know, but the realisation struck her nonetheless: she'd had her fill of bullies and bigmouths this week, and now without the shackles of a career plan and the hierarchy of management to hold her back she unloaded all her pent-up anger and resentment on Boot Camp Dan. Yes, was the answer. She knew exactly who he was and she proceeded to let him know, in no uncertain terms.

'Are you still filming? Stop, stop at once!' but James's cries were again ignored by Surjit. Not only had he left the camera filming, he was now moving closer, framing a nice head-and-shoulders close-up of the two combatants: this is awesome, this is so good it'll get on television for sure, thought Surjit – correctly as it turned out, just not in the way he imagined.

In Aberdeenshire, Mother cackled with delight at the confrontation – the small woman dressed like a *Downton Abbey* gamekeeper threw about words like *bully, thug* and *misogynist,* and as for the muscleman that Pamela lusted after, he looked ready to explode and – ooh – the language he used, you'd never hear that this time in the morning on *Homes Under the Hammer.* Pamela, shocked by Boot Camp Dan's change of character and concerned his outburst would give Mother another one of her turns, reached across to snap down the lid of her laptop, but Mother was quick and blocked her, she didn't want to miss a thing. At the opposite end of the country James Doyle finally wrestled the camera away from eager young Surjit and peered down the barrel to address everyone at home. 'Just a technical hitch folks. Join us at ten thirty for our proper big live launch.' Then James jabbed the off button furiously – show over.

CHAPTER **FOUR**

PADDY BROKE AWAY FROM HIS CONVERSATION at the sight of his returning, rather bedraggled sister. 'Monica, what's happened?'

Filled with resentment, Monica eyed the miscreant Border terrier Winkle, who remained totally oblivious to the chaos he'd created. He turned twice on the spot then sat at Paddy's feet, settled down and continued his ablutions, hoiking his leg up over his shoulder.

Comedy Tim looked up from his screen. 'Here, you can take this seat, I need to go,' he said trousering the phone and sloping off back towards the park.

Monica, grateful for the seat, flopped into it, let out a dramatic sigh, then recounted her chance meeting with Boot Camp Dan, not missing out a single expletive. Paddy, Hazel and Kenton sat stunned by every word. Winkle gave his nether regions a noisy slurp.

'Absolute pig of a human being,' said the man leaning against the Munster's serving hatch when Monica finished. Monica blinked at the stranger, a small stocky man with his ginger hair clipped in a short buzzcut, and recalled him: Pete the birdwatcher.

'Ever since he turned up here he's been nothing but trouble.'

The dogwalkers nodded their silent agreement, and Pete, warming to his subject, continued. 'For nearly twenty years we had our clubhouse down on the peninsula. It was the best place for miles around to birdwatch; we won awards for the quality of our hide and our contribution to the environment. He was here a month, and we got moved.'

'How?' asked Monica, not noticing the death stares and head shakes of the dogwalkers behind him, each one of them suggesting it was a conversational avenue to walk straight past, but Monica was not one to pick up on subtle social cues and persisted. 'How could he do that if you were established?'

'He'd found some obscure byelaw and used it to bully and browbeat the manager at the Visitors' Centre into agreeing with him. My daughter, Alison, she works in the café there, she says he's as weak as water. Boot Camp Dan basically bullied him into moving us on. As a compromise,' Pete gave invisible finger quotes around the last word to highlight his contempt for it, 'he found us a new spot for our clubhouse. Tucked in the far corner of the car park. Miles away from the river, no views as such, not a bird to be seen.'

'Doesn't sound fair to me, Pete,' sympathised Paddy.

'It's people like him that make me wish I was back in the regiment,' said Pete. 'I used to be a sniper, did I tell you that? Gulf War One.' Paddy shook his head in response. 'I'd love to have my old rifle back. Accurate over a kilometre.'

Monica and Paddy exchanged a nervous glance, but Pete hadn't finished. 'From here, it'd be a cinch.' Pete extended a stiff straight left arm before him, and curled his right hand in front of his face. With his left eye closed tight his imaginary rifle was complete. His tongue clicked to playact the chamber being loaded and again as the bolt was drawn back, then: 'Pew!' he fired. 'The bullet'll hit him before he's even heard the shot,' said Pete. 'Travelling at two and a half thousand feet a second, the bullet would hit his skull and—' Pete clenched a fist then flared it open, spreading his fingers wide apart. 'Bosh! It'd explode like a squashed tomato!'

Monica and Paddy's exchanged glances became even more nervous. Pete looked at them nonplussed, nothing else to add.

'Sounds like you've given it a lot of thought, Pete.' Paddy used a jokey tone, hoping to raise the mood.

'Passes the time,' replied Pete in all seriousness, missing the jocularity. 'Anyway, must go.' He lifted his bacon roll from the serving hatch and raised his cup in salute. 'See you later.'

Pete's contribution killed the mood. The dogwalkers all stood, gathered up their respective leashes, agreed with each other to catch up soon but no-one felt the need to specify when; all wanting some time alone.

PADDY TRUDGED THE PERIMETER of the Riverside Conservation Park following a different route to normal.

He'd lost sight of his fellow dogwalkers, in fact he couldn't see another soul: no joggers, no psychopathic birdwatchers, not even a seagull. To say it had turned quiet was an understatement, even the dogs were muted and disinterested; they plodded forwards, eyes, ears and tails down, barely a glance exchanged between them. His mind wandered; his dream life took over. In his own internal fantasy, the crowd swayed and pounded to the amplified sound, the electric beats and the echoing bass. Paddy stood before them, their leader, the mixing desk his altar: Paddy the superstar DJ. With every beat the revellers moved as one, writhing as a wave, following the music beneath a barrage of laser-lights illuminating the Ibizan night sky. Hordes of clubbers, pilgrims flocking from every corner of Europe and beyond, entranced by the music he curated with the artistry and inspiration of a master. Thousands of devoted eyes looked up at him in adoration every single night as he took the microphone: 'Party people in the house, are you ready to—'

He stopped dead. It wasn't a daydream. He could hear loud, up-tempo, high-energy dance music, and it was coming from nearby. He flicked the leashes to turn the dogs in the direction of the music and went to investigate.

JAMES DOYLE HAD INSTRUCTED the techie boy Surjit to find the fastest, bounciest, most upbeat high-tempo dance tune out there, and play it at maximum volume. James had discussed it with Boot Camp Dan: *if we want to draw a line under the earlier fiasco, we need to go big and we need to go bold; the music needs to be faster, the jokes need to be sharper and the outfit needs to be tighter.*

Surjit counted down the techie crew, 'Three ... two ... one. We're live!' and pressed "Play". The music started. The lighting rigs burst into bright brilliant colour. The grey-suited investors squirmed uncomfortably in their seats, unused to such loud music so early in the morning; and all around every last living creature whether mammal, bird or fish fled the area as fast as they could, deafened and bewildered by the sudden assault on their senses. The people in the park looked around, unable to understand why the Glastonbury Festival had suddenly come to town unannounced.

In Aberdeenshire, Pamela logged in to her ancient laptop with eager anticipation, just like all of the other Boot Camp Dan fans nationwide: in big neon letters the words *"Live from the Riverside Country Park"* filled the screen; the music pulsed through her laptop's tinny little speaker, so loud it was distorted with crackles and vibrations.

'Mother, come and sit down, it's starting.'

'Ladies and gentleman,' declared a voice over the top of the music, 'Are you ready to work those bodies? Here's ...' the word was held for several seconds like a Las Vegas prize-fight announcer to add the showbiz razzamatazz, 'Boot Camp Dan!'

Surjit zoomed his camera to the back of the stage, framing a nice shot for the spectacle about to happen; James Doyle had commanded everything they had be thrown into the opening. Fixing his camera position, the confetti cannons, originally intended to close the show, fired. Thousands of golden paper petals filled the area, fluttering down, awaiting the entrance of Boot Camp Dan. Surjit kept the camera steady; from the commands in his earpiece, he knew that in less than a second the curtain would rise and Boot Camp Dan would stride through like the undefeated heavyweight champion of the world to do his thing.

Sure enough, the curtain rose, smoothly and fluidly, but Boot Camp Dan was not standing there waiting like a gladiator. Driven by instinct and reflex Surjit lowered the camera's gaze and zoomed in at the broken, bloodied remains on the floor. Boot Camp Dan had been defeated. The dumbbell used to split his skull apart was wedged deep into the hole it had created; its polished chrome sparkled under the beam of the stage lighting. Golden petals of confetti stuck to the thick viscous blood and brain matter oozing from his open head wound.

In a small sitting room in Aberdeenshire an elderly lady heard her daughter, a woman of almost retirement age, sob.

CHAPTER **FIVE**

NEEDLESS TO SAY THE LIVE LAUNCH WAS CANCELLED – again – which came as a disappointment to some. Surjit the techie however, was not among them. Spotting his opportunity, he thrust his camera into the face of every person he could, instantly asked their reactions, and promptly sold the footage to each reporter arriving to cover the incident. Surjit found it ironic: Boot Camp Dan had always promised the exposure Surjit would get from him was worth much more in the long run than a few quid to compensate his cold toes on all those mornings. Surjit had made sure Boot Camp Dan came good on that promise by going home several thousand pounds richer, a clutch of new contacts into news studios all across the country and the promise of an internship at *Lorraine*. All in all the day hadn't ended badly for Surjit.

For James Doyle, by contrast, all in all the day had ended very badly. Time is money and not wishing to waste either the investors scattered like startled crows before the police turned up. With grim realisation James knew his business and investment lay smashed to pieces on the floor. Then, to add insult to injury, he later discovered an expensive scrape the full length of his new Mercedes thanks to a belligerent TV van convinced it could fit into a space at least a third of its width too narrow. The van promptly scarpered at the sight of sparks and the sound of crunching metal, and by conveniently "forgetting" to leave any insurance details it just about crowned the perfect day for James.

Monica found James sat on the corner of the stage: *he's not doing anything, maybe this is my chance to pitch my business to him,* wondered Monica. Then her self-awareness caught up with her ambition and she realised it was probably not the right time nor place. He looked shattered: elbows on knees, head in hands. She settled a few feet along from him; *keep it respectable and professional, Monica.* Seeing him appear so drained and traumatised made her uncomfortable: *should I put an arm across his shoulder, only to comfort him, nothing else, I don't want anything misconstrued or taken out of context, I feel for him, he seems a nice guy, he stood up to Boot Camp Dan when he was going berserk at me.* As her inner turmoil pondered the MeToo dilemma James realised she was there. He faced her, gave a weak smile then flopped his head back down again.

'Are you okay?' she asked, desperately wishing she could think of something better to say: *where's Paddy, he finds this kind of thing so much easier than me?*

'I honestly don't know.' James sounded tired and weary. 'I'm going to have to make a lot of phone calls if I'm to get any credibility back with the investors.'

It wasn't the answer she was expecting, her question aimed more at his general wellbeing and state of mind, but she gave a comforting 'Hmmm' and let it go. He rose to his feet and started to shuffle away. In a tired voice he bid her farewell but she didn't hear; across the park a flurry of new activity had caught her attention.

PADDY AND THE DOGWALKERS had congregated near the Visitors' Centre, but were still not allowed inside, the police having commandeered it for their on-site operational base. Instead, they lingered at the car park's edge and watched the events unfurl. First, they saw the ambulance arrive, then the uniformed police officers and then the TV and radio crews, whilst at the same time and in the opposite direction the investors stampeded to their big luxury cars and dispersed as fast as they could.

None of them wanted to admit it, but they were finding it quite a thrill.

'I'd better go find Monica,' Paddy said after a while, realising he'd not seen her for at least an hour. In fact, now he came to think of it, he'd not seen her since coming back from her Boot Camp Dan altercation. Suddenly concerned for her wellbeing, he rose from the low railing he was perched against ready to head off in search of her.

'Hold on, who's this?' Hazel's words prompted him to look in the same direction as her, at a young woman in a plum trouser suit coming towards them from the direction of the Visitors' Centre. She walked with a confidence that Paddy found attractive. Her skin was warm brown and her tied-back hair was glossy black; her face long, angular and striking.

She made eye contact with Paddy, never blinking: 'My name is Detective Constable Nicci Sharma. Are you Mr Mountain?'

'Minton. Patrick Minton,' Paddy clarified. An uncomfortable itch nibbled at his arms; the way she stared at him in silent scrutiny.

'I'd like to ask you a few questions if I may?'

Paddy nodded, and studied her with more interest; she was certainly attractive but there was something else, something familiar ... bingo!

'Did you say Sharma? You're not Dev Sharma's sister, are you? I was at school with Dev, he was in my class. How is he?'

The hard stare thawed immediately and the stiff shoulders relaxed. 'You know Dev? He's good. He's a quantity surveyor now, lives in London with his wife, baby number two on the way.'

'Nice. Good for him.' His reply was genuine. 'Please send him my best regards, will you? Tell him Paddy Minton says hello?'

'Wait ... Paddy? Paddy Minton? Oh my god!' Her hands shot up in animated reaction, cupping her mouth. The rigid imposing attitude was gone, replaced instead by a giddy fangirl. 'We all used to have such crushes on you, everybody did.' Paddy tried restraining the famous smile, but failed. The detective noticed. Deep inside a quiver of electricity last felt a decade ago flickered, its return exciting and not unwelcome, transporting her immediately back to the school gates. 'So, how've you been? You're looking good, I mean well, you're looking well.'

Flattery and adoration seemed to be a good distraction: Paddy's concerns for Monica completely disappeared.

'Who'd have thought, after all these years?' continued DC Sharma breathlessly. 'I still remember you on the school trip to Brittany. That was great, wasn't it?'

Paddy grinned, never breaking his warm eye contact with her, but internally the miniature curator inside his head frantically rifled through cabinets, rummaged through cupboards and upended drawers in a desperate hunt for any clues: he found the dimmest recollection of a fumble with someone below decks on the cross-channel ferry and the taste of Juicy Fruit chewing gum, could it be ...?

'That's right, you were in Dev's class,' she continued, lost in halcyon nostalgia, 'and I was in the year above. You had a sister, didn't you?'

'Still do.'

'She was in my class. Can I be frank? I remember her being a bit hoity-toity, a bit too full of herself, a bit stuck up.'

Conflict swept across Paddy's conscience: chivalry stepped forwards and told him, *"Defend your sister, be a gentleman,"* but enjoying basking in past glories and adoration, honesty popped up and said, *"Steady on pal, don't spoil things and anyway ... maybe she's got a point."*

'So, what's she doing now?'

'What's who doing now?' asked Monica.

THERE WAS A REASON why the Visitors' Centre resembled an old barn. It's because it was. Except there'd never been a barn on that site in the whole of history, it was a riverside wetland, why would there be a barn? At great expense the local council had procured an old sixteenth-century barn from Suffolk and had it dismantled: every beam numbered, every timber catalogued. Then transported here, where it was reassembled like an Ikea wardrobe. To be fair, it was money well spent: it looked the part and blended nicely into the surrounding landscape. From an untidy, neglected spit of common land by the river emerged a rustic idyll loved and enjoyed by the community. The low-lying spring sun hovered behind Monica's shoulder as she sat on the edge of the stage. It offered a brief respite from the cold, damp day and warmed her back nicely. Ahead of her, about the length of a football pitch distant, she watched as the sunlight gave the ancient oak timbers a warm honey glow; they radiated against the grey sky. Then she noticed the activity and her curiosity was well and truly piqued. She watched the arrival of the young woman, noting her brusque command of uniformed beat bobbies, sending them running in all directions from the Visitors' Centre. Then she saw her approaching Paddy and felt the need to intervene: *Paddy's sweet and well-meaning, but he's Peter Pan, the boy that never grew up, I need to take charge, he needs a responsible adult to keep him out of trouble,* she decided.

Monica's first impressions changed as she neared her brother: the young woman who'd marched across the park, hard as nails, like a battlefield general bossing orders to the uniformed beat bobbies, was now perched on the bonnet of a police car with her hands pressed between her thighs. This wasn't the first time Monica had seen grown women revert to giddy schoolgirls, and she was certain it wouldn't be the last: *not again, Paddy, why do you always do this?*

'So, what's she doing now?' asked the young woman with, Monica noticed, beautifully manicured eyebrows.

'What's who doing now?' asked Monica with the deliberate intent of disrupting the cosy tête-à-tête.

The woman stiffened at the interruption. Her head snapped sharply across to face Monica full-on. She rose to her feet, her posture erect and strictly business; her eyes re-engaged work mode, never blinking: *how does she get her eyebrows so perfect, how come mine never go like that?*

'Hey Mon, there you are,' Paddy beckoned with a scooping gesture. 'Look who's here, remember, from school? Nicci—'

'Detective Constable Sharma,' the steel in her voice made Paddy recoil in surprise, 'I would like to ask a few questions ... of both of you, in fact, as I understand you were present at the scene?'

'No, not quite,' replied Monica, the snap in her tone matching that of her inquisitor. It had taken a while but the penny had finally dropped, she did indeed remember Nikhitha Sharma from school, more's the pity. Flashbacks of the catty gang of cool girls trying to get Paddy's attention: *sometimes pretending to be my friend just to wangle an invite back home to try to get close to him, always a bit hoity-toity, a bit too full of themselves, a bit stuck up.*

A warm sensation rushed through Monica's veins, not entirely unpleasant, and with an undisguised glee she was happy to prove DC Sharma wrong and chalk up a point against her. 'We only arrived after everyone screamed, plenty of other people were at the scene before us.'

'Yes, thank you, I am aware of that.' A forced politeness kept the frustration at bay. 'And they have been or will be spoken with separately. But I understand there was bad feeling between you two and the victim, is that correct?' Monica and Paddy both shook their heads in denial. 'Okay,' replied Sharma in a neutral voice that neither believed or disbelieved them. She made a note in a small pocketbook that they couldn't read from where they stood, then asked, 'Can you think of anyone that may have wanted to murder Boot Camp Dan?'

'So, you're saying it's definitely murder?' asked Monica.

'Unless he was a particularly clumsy juggler, I think it's safe to assume someone other than himself or gravity embedded a heavy barbell in the back of his head.' Sharma couldn't hide her delight in volleying a jibe back to little Miss Snooty, game on: one-all.

'Dumbbell.' Monica noticed Sharma's reaction and took pride in the veiled insult. 'Dumbbell. That's the proper name for a handheld weight. A barbell is a long one that you hold in both hands.' Game, set and match Miss Minton.

'No, we don't,' Paddy confirmed. 'We didn't have much to do with him at all. We weren't invited to his stage show, we don't know who killed him and to be honest we don't even know who called the police.'

'And yet here you are,' added Monica.

'And here we are.' Nicci Sharma twitched a finger and two uniformed constables appeared, seemingly from nowhere. 'Take their statements,' she commanded. 'I want a full account from each of them from the moment they woke up this morning.'

The constables took a step forward, but a man's voice stopped them in their tracks. 'Not so fast, people.'

The constables and the Mintons turned in unison towards Nicci Sharma, seeking some clarity. Instead, they caught her rolling her eyes heavenwards and tutting.

'No,' she muttered in a voice little more than a whisper. 'They can't have sent him?'

SO, IF ANYONE WAS KEEPING SCORE, it was a day of definite winners and definite losers. The biggest loser, Boot Camp Dan aside of course, was probably James by a long lead. But the biggest winner? Young Surjit was quite some way ahead: cashing in on all the exposure Boot Camp Dan had promised, admittedly never expecting it to be at his own expense like this, but nonetheless he'd come good and delivered for Surjit in the end. However, in fact, the actual winner of the day was the Munsters': with the Visitors' Centre closed off as the police's on-site centre of operations, legions of hungry news crews caught out of doors and far from home followed by a second and then third wave of uniformed police officers, all tired with cold, wet feet and in dire need of sustenance, descended on the grotty little cabin. The Munsters' biohazard by the river scored its best day ever; Mr Munster even cracked a smile, breaking the habit of a lifetime, although it began to hurt after a few minutes so he gave up.

As for Detective Constable Nicci Sharma, she was undecided into whose camp she fell. On the one hand it was good – very good – to meet up with Paddy Minton after all these years, and still get the same giddy thrill; on the other hand, she could not believe who the top brass had foisted on her murder investigation: *why me, what have I done to deserve this?*

CHAPTER **SIX**

WHEN THE SMALL MAN IN THE BEIGE RAINCOAT bellowed and blustered his way into the conversation, the constables and the *We Sit Pets* team of dogwalkers looked to Nicci Sharma for clarity. She instead just rolled her eyes with disbelief and contempt. With a tilt of the head she indicated towards the Visitors' Centre and began to walk. The man in the raincoat, taking the hint, followed her. Within seconds they were through the door and out of sight, talking in private. Left outside on the field, the constables didn't know what they were meant to do next. They looked at each other for comfort and advice; afraid to disturb the raised voices coming from within.

'Shall we go home and await your phone call?' suggested Paddy.

Looks of confusion and bewilderment passed between the constables.

Paddy pushed his advantage: 'Okay, see you later.'

The constables bid them a cheery farewell then, for want of anything better to do, joined the end of a very long queue at the Munsters' cabin. By the time they eventually reached the front they were met with the bitter disappointment that Mr Munster had run out of KitKats. Crushed that they had to go without, they took their coffees and sulked, completely forgetting all about the dogwalkers they were meant to be tending.

THE *WE SIT PETS* CONTINGENT of dogwalkers congregated at the mouth of the car park. With the sudden screech of tyres and brakes, a small camper van pulled up alongside them. The driver, a small man in a very ordinary plain sweatshirt and blue jeans, hopped out.

'Pete?' said Paddy, taking a moment to recognise him out of his camouflage. 'Where've you been?'

'Yes, you've missed all the excitement,' added Hazel.

Pete's eyes darted left and right, scanning all around. 'I came back. There was something I wanted to get out of the clubhouse.'

Paddy's attention shifted and Monica followed his gaze: in the furthest corner of the car park sat a rather dishevelled timber cabin. Rot bubbled under the layers of dark brown paint and the flat roof sagged with a worrying belly. A single narrow slit of a shutter was flipped closed, suggesting nobody was home; the moss and grime all around the edges of the shutter suggested nobody had been home for some time. Monica couldn't blame them: it looked the dingiest dungeon of a place. Without realising it, Monica had taken two paces back, just in case rising damp was contagious. Aside from three pigeons on the roof of a Royal Mail van tearing apart a discarded burger, there wasn't another bird anywhere to be seen. Monica could appreciate why the birdwatchers were so disappointed about being relocated, and looking at the state of that cabin it'd seem the membership had fallen too; *no wonder Pete's angry*, she thought.

'What did you forget, Pete?' asked Paddy.

Pete seemed confused by Paddy's simple question: 'You ... what?'

'I'll give you a hand, I've always fancied seeing what's inside there,' offered Paddy helpfully. Pete's eyes didn't stop flicking left to right and back again, never settling.

Activity was all around them: police officers, journalists and other people linked to the investigation milled about everywhere; vehicles arrived, vehicles left, vehicles unloaded, vehicles reloaded.

'Ah ... no ... actually, I've just remembered what I've done with it. Okay. Must go.'

He hopped back in the camper van, and fired up the engine. It rattled like a box of spanners before pulling away from the kerb with a sudden lurch. That left the pet-sitters: Paddy, Monica, Comedy Tim, Hazel, and a dozen dogs who'd grown bored and hungry with so much hanging around. They'd begun nibbling and snapping at each other to pass the time.

A whippet on receipt of a nipped ear gave a pained yelp. 'I'd better get these chaps home,' said Tim in response, bidding them farewell and heading for his car, a battered and beaten old Peugeot: a nasty rust patch bubbled around the back wheel, bearing an uncanny resemblance to the map of Crete.

'It's been a strange morning, hasn't it,' mulled Paddy. 'So, tell me Monica, is this how your corporate launch events usually end up?'

'I've been to worse,' she replied with a tone implying *ask a silly question ...*

Paddy didn't notice and continued ruminating. 'I wonder who that was in the raincoat?'

'I was wondering that too,' replied Monica. 'He must be important; the way they all jumped at his every word.'

'I think he sold my daughter her endowment mortgage,' added Hazel, followed by 'What?' when she saw the aghast faces of the Mintons bearing back at her.

'It's a murder enquiry not a credit check. Whatever next? There's been an armed robbery at the bank: let's see if Greggs the Bakers has anyone they can spare to investigate?'

Hazel looked crestfallen, even her jaunty cap had gone flat. 'No, I guess not. You're probably right.'

Probably? screamed the questioning voice inside Monica's head but, recognising Hazel's humiliation and feeling a tinge of guilt, for once she had the social awareness not to say it aloud. Instead, she responded, 'I daresay we'll find out in due course.'

'I can ask Nicci, if you like?' Paddy offered. He clasped her stiff white business card between two fingers, and hoped Monica would give him a plausible excuse to call DC Sharma.

If Monica was unimpressed by Nicci Sharma's attempts to get Paddy's attention when they were at school together, she was even less so now. 'That won't be necessary, thank you, Patrick.'

Paddy gave Monica a gentle kiss on the cheek and promised to call her later. He began preparing his dogs for their journeys home; all the while the little processor in the back of his head whirred silently away, looking for a reason to give DC Sharma a call.

'SO, WHAT'S THE word on the street? Does the vic have a name? And do we have a perp yet?'

Detective Constable Nicci Sharma sighed inwardly. Professionalism tried hard not to let the disgust show: *best poker face required, I can't believe they've sent him.*

'We have identified the vic-*tim* as a Mr Daniel Usborne, otherwise known as Boot Camp Dan,' she replied once she'd calmed her turbulent thoughts, 'and no, we have not identified any possible suspects yet.'

The small man adopted a stance that looked well-rehearsed: feet shoulder-width apart, both hands stuffed in his trouser pockets, the tail of his beige raincoat pinned behind his wrists, flapping behind him in a cinematic way. *Definitely very Pacino*, he thought, catching his reflection against the window.

'We need this wrapped up fast,' he said. 'Can't have the public afraid to visit the park. Not on my manor. I don't want the press on my back over this. I've promised to have this closed in twenty-four hours, forty-eight tops.'

Nicci Sharma gave another inward sigh, hoping this would be over soon and she could get back to work on *her* murder inquiry.

'Is there anything else, Inspector Canning?' but she only asked the question because it was expected of her, she'd already begun walking.

'No. Carry on,' he replied to the back of her exiting head. 'I'll inspect the scene here,' he said to an empty room.

OUTSIDE NICCI SHARMA recognised a friendly face – or at least part of one. The eyes of the forensic lead widened in recognition, and even though the rest of her face was hidden by a paper mask inside a paper hood Nicci knew she was smiling.

'I'm in the right place, then,' she said by way of greeting. Two colleagues had gathered beside her, also clad tip to toe in white paper. 'What can you tell me about the victim so far, Nicci?'

The three white-hooded heads lined up together like a mountain range and listened to Nicci Sharma's summary of the scene: 'Daniel Michael Usborne, otherwise known as Boot Camp Dan. Caucasian male, thirty-three years old. Personal trainer so he was physically fit and strong. Discovered on the outdoor stage over there when the curtain was raised for his big entrance.' She noticed the eyebrows raise inside the hoods. 'Yes, yes, very showbiz. Anyway, his head had been stoved in with one of his weights. We've left it in situ, so the pleasure of extracting it can be all yours. He was discovered at approximately ten thirty-three this morning by ... well, everyone in attendance for his live show.'

'Thanks. And we'll need samples from anyone who has been near to the victim this morning,' said the forensic lead; her offsiders rustled their agreement.

'Leave it to me, I'll get them across to you,' she promised and cast her eyes from side to side, scanning the horizon. 'But I don't know where any of them have gone.'

And with that brief summing up, Nicci Sharma bid them farewell and began to walk away. 'Right, I'll let you crack on with it, see you later.'

'Wait, aren't you the Senior Investigating Officer? That's what it said on the ticket.'

'There's been a change of plan.' Nicci Sharma struggled, and failed, to keep the disappointment out of her voice. 'They've assigned Inspector Canning as SIO instead.'

The reaction to her news was all too visible. The collective white suits all crumpled and dropped in despair, as though an avalanche rocked the mountain range. 'You're joking? Not *Law-and-Order* Canning? Seriously?'

'Seriously. And he's in there waiting for you. Have fun.' And with that she left the white masks turning the air blue.

A TEN-MINUTE SEARCH of the area finally yielded her two wayward constables: they lurked in the furthest corner of the park, looking out at the distant land across the water on the horizon. They were still grumbling about missing out on the last KitKat.

'Where've they gone?' demanded Nicci Sharma.

'Sold them all,' replied the first copper, called Caffrey. He was a young lad, with short ginger curls and the last blooms of teenage acne.

'What? No. Not the KitKats. The people I asked you to talk to. Where are they?'

'Oh. Them,' replied the second copper, a heavyset, veteran of many years called Perkins. 'Don't know. But he's got Twix if you want one of them instead?'

'They've all gone home. They said you can call them if you wanted them,' added young Caffrey, thinking he was helping.

'I can call them, can I? And did you make a note of their phone numbers for me?'

'Errr ...' was all the youngster could manage to respond.

'Did we?' asked Perkins the malingerer rhetorically. This was his forte, a skill he'd honed over many years: do nothing but be quick-witted enough to get away with it. Detective Constable Sharma knew from painful previous experience Perkins was already crafting an elaborate justification why it was everybody else's fault except his.

She walked off with a dismissive 'pah' and a dissenting flap of the hand, carried on a cloud of rage and fury.

Young Caffrey, only on the job a few months, felt the uneasy ripple of anxiety shiver through him as he watched his superior officer stomping off in a huff. 'What do we do now?'

'Well, I don't know about you, my young friend,' the heavy old skiver rose to a standing position with great effort, and gave a theatrical stretch of the arms, 'but all this talking has made me hungry. I quite fancy that Twix now. Come on, you're buying.'

CHAPTER **SEVEN**

'DID THE POLICE CONTACT YOU?' PADDY ASKED no-one in particular but everyone in general. The heads around the table shook and muttered no.

The morning sun struggled to peer through a low grey cloud, and looked on the verge of giving up. A damp hung on the air. The Munsters' had no record queues today, and definitely no smiles. Instead, the heavy monobrow behind the hatch looked very serious.

Normal service resumed, including: 'Yuk, flowery, must be yours.' Paddy swapped the tea in his hand with the one in Monica's then grabbed the least damp chair for himself, leaving Monica a choice: stand or wet bum.

'Are we off the hook?' asked Hazel.

Monica shot her a look that asked more questions than she was prepared to say aloud and responded with, 'It just means they've not got around to taking our statements, that's all,' but no, she couldn't hold it back any longer: 'Off the hook? Really? Who do you think you are, Reggie Kray?'

Paddy, always the people-pleaser, sought a ceasefire. 'Whoa whoa. That's enough, all of you, come on. It's a tough time for all of us—'

'He's not wrong, you know,' came a different voice, the source being Comedy Tim. He felt all eyes upon him, so he peeled his own away from the phone screen and faced his audience. 'I mean, the miserable old devil's dead and we're still sitting out here!'

A bank of solemn faces looked back. The coarse caw of a lonely seagull was the only sound breaking the silence.

With hand gestures and a flippant tone of voice, Tim demanded, 'What? Too soon?' Nobody responded; cue another awkward silence. 'What? You never liked him, no-one did. So, all of you, stop pretending you're upset, you bunch of hypocrites.'

'Hey,' Paddy's rebuttal came hard and fast. 'Firstly, I wasn't talking about Boot Camp Dan. I meant it's a tough time for us, all of us, because we have to live with the fallout: seeing the mess he was in, facing the police and all that.' Paddy's voice started to trail away, losing confidence in his own argument, and hoping nobody asked him what comes second.

Thankfully Tim was still venting his outrage. 'Everyone hated him. He's only got himself to blame. In fact, I'm amazed it never happened sooner.'

Kenton had been sitting as always with the still composure of a statue. He began to nod. 'I hate to say it but he's right. He was a nasty piece of work. Always had been. I first knew him when he was twelve years old and even then he was an arrogant, mean, son of a—'

'I didn't know you had history with him,' interrupted Hazel, just as he was getting to the good bit. 'How so?'

'Boxing, he was actually a very good middleweight, could've made it big, until ...' Everyone leaned in, keen to hear until what, but Kenton's eyes rose upwards as if trying to see behind him, to catch a glimpse of the past. A moment or two in the real world but a lifetime later in his head he continued, 'He was quite handy at judo and kick-boxing too. I'd heard he was trying to make it as a cage fighter doing the mixed martial arts, but then he turned up here about nine months ago and made everyone's life a misery.'

The dogwalkers nodded in silent agreement, each one of them having at some point been on the receiving end of Boot Camp Dan's ire, each one of them banished from the nice Visitors' Centre café on his orders.

'He certainly wasn't an easy man to get along with,' admitted Hazel; cue more silent nods from the group, 'but it's wrong, wicked, to make jokes like that, Tim,' cue yet more silent nods from the group. Tim, in no mood for criticism and certainly in no mood for apologies, stood up. He startled his dogs with an aggressive jerk of their leashes and walked off without a word. Monica, seeing an opportunity, darted straight into his newly vacated seat.

'What?' she demanded of the aghast faces staring at her; it was still warm, bliss.

Attention wasn't held on her very long though due to an unfamiliar voice surprising them from behind. 'I thought I might find you all here.'

Detective Constable Nicci Sharma, owner of the voice, approached, her fists balled into the pockets of a light rain jacket. 'I'm glad you're all together. I need to take your statements from yesterday and then someone will be along soon to take your fingerprints, is that okay?'

'Why's everyone looking at me?' Monica wondered, then remembered it was only a few days since she'd offered to take care of all their admin. Trying on the invisible crown of leadership, and rather liking the feel of it, Monica responded in a loud, clear voice that she and *her staff* would be more than happy to co-operate with the police enquiries. Her surreptitious glance swept the congregation, but nobody appeared to react to the comment: *how quickly have they delegated every last decision over to me?*

Nicci Sharma dismissed Kenton immediately, on the grounds he wasn't even there when it happened. Hazel was dispatched with great speed too: being a lady of more mature years, stiff joints and a weak pelvic floor, Hazel made clear without any delicacy why she doesn't run for any reason, and certainly why she doesn't lift heavy weights above her head: *if I'd run over there, and raised his metal thingy, you'd be mopping me off the floor as well as him, and you can check that with my doctor if you like.* Nicci Sharma assured her that wouldn't be necessary.

'And, another thing,' Hazel hadn't finished her statement for the defence, 'there was a young man with a video camera annoying people. He kept sticking it in front of people's faces. The first I knew about Boot Camp Dan being killed was when he blocked my path, told me on camera and straight away asked me for my reaction. I gave him a proper piece of my mind for being so insensitive, I can tell you. You'll see that on his recording.'

Nicci Sharma didn't mention she'd spent the night poring over the hours of footage taken by Surjit and his associates. She knew before she'd even spoken to her that Hazel was one of the last he'd interviewed and she'd seemed genuinely taken aback and horrified. DC Sharma thanked Hazel for her time, and let her go.

'Come and join us, Nicci,' beckoned Paddy. He and Monica had remained at the table beside the Munsters' cabin. 'I'll get you a tea, come and sit yourself down.'

She took a seat and immediately felt self-conscious. Her status had changed: no longer the authority figure controlling the situation. As she tipped a tight-lipped awkward smile to Monica she realised she'd become the shy girl desperate to make a good impression in front of the boy-she-liked's family. She closed her eyes and took a long breath: slowly drawing up through the nose, releasing a slow exhale through the mouth, desperately seeking composure. Then Paddy sat beside her and any composure followed the slow exhale, and got lost on the breeze.

'Here you go.' Paddy placed three cups on the table, one for everyone.

A sip, a wince: 'Yuk, flowery. Must be yours,' he said, swapping the one he held for the one in front of Monica.

Monica took it, and dropped a hint. 'Hopefully we'll be allowed in the nice café soon?'

Nicci spotted it and replied, 'We're almost finished here. We should be releasing the Visitors' Centre back to its operators around lunchtime.'

'How long have you been in the police, Nicci?' asked Paddy.

Should I be having conversations like this with potential suspects, pondered Detective Constable Sharma, but then she got the Paddy smile and replied, 'Six years this summer. Nearly four in uniform, then became a detective about two years ago.'

'That's great.' Paddy's reply sounded as genuine as always, it gave her comfort for lowering her guard. 'And now you're running the show, brilliant.'

Nicci Sharma's expression gave an answer of its own, but still she responded with a single word: 'Hardly.'

As soon as the word left her lips, regret sunk an inward groan: *I shouldn't have said that.*

'Everything okay?' asked Monica.

Nicci took a pause, then said, 'This was meant to be my case. They'd promised me. The next murder, it'll be mine, my first. Instead, they gave it to *him*.'

'Who?' replied Paddy, thinking back to the day before. 'Do you mean the small guy in the raincoat?'

'Yes. They gave my case to DI Canning,' Nicci held a finger below her nose and shot her eyes to the sky, a reflex reaction to stifle emotion. 'Know what they call him behind his back? *Law-and-Order* Canning.'

'Why's that?' Monica was fascinated. 'Is he the old-school, no-holds-barred, bring-back-the-death-penalty sort?'

Nicci snorted a laugh that erupted from a place of surprise, 'No. It's because he's an idiot.' She could tell they didn't understand. 'He's a joke, everyone laughs at him behind his back. He's not a proper copper, he's only been in the job six months.'

'But you said he was a detective inspector?'

'He's fast-tracked. Direct entry. Some nitwit in the Home Office had an idea to invite people in from other careers and industries, drop them straight in at senior management positions.'

'Where'd he come from?'

'You won't believe this, he was a building society assistant manager, selling mortgages and pensions.'

Monica's corporate mode switched on. 'That doesn't seem the most obvious of skill transfers.'

'I'm glad you see how ridiculous it is. He's got no experience for this kind of work.'

'But, *Law and Order*?'

'They call him that because he watches telly to see how to be a copper. Rather than ask us, who've been in the field, been there, seen it, done it, he uses old TV shows instead. You saw him barging on to the scene yesterday, strutting about, acting like a maverick tough talking New York cop with a twenty-four-hour deadline from the DA. He's a total joke.'

'But, if he's such a laughing stock, why's he been given this case?' asked Paddy.

'Oh, Paddy,' replied Monica, 'he's a man. He probably drinks with the right people, plays in the right golf club.' Nicci Sharma nodded in agreement, Monica had hit the nail square on the head. 'Why do you think I gave up a well-paid job in the City to walk dogs?' For Nicci's benefit, Monica shared her experience with Martin the Ignoramus, and although they didn't realise it at the time their shared experiences brought them a little bit closer.

TEAS DRUNK, CHIT-CHAT OVER, it was time to get back to work, Nicci away, Detective Constable Sharma present. With a small digital recorder placed on the table and a notebook in hand, she asked the Minton siblings their movements leading up to the discovery of Boot Camp Dan's demise in a shower of golden confetti. Her first impressions were that their accounts sounded pretty robust and convincing, but she knew it was her responsibility to challenge every single aspect of it thoroughly, no matter what her personal feelings suggested. She listened, she made notes, but she didn't pass comment or make judgment, until:

'Arch-enemy?'

'That's right. My arch-enemy. My nemesis. The Joker to my Batman. The ... Monica, who's Superman's arch-enemy?'

'I don't know, the Penguin?'

'No, that's Batman again. I need me a supervillain—'

'You're Superman?' Monica asked with an incredulous giggle. She noticed the way Nicci Sharma was watching them, and she dropped the levity from her voice. 'I'm afraid my brother is a little prone to dramatics. What he is trying to say is Boot Camp Dan was a difficult character to get on with, and there were one or two personality clashes between him and Paddy, that's all. Nothing to worry about.'

DC Sharma gave an 'uh-huh' that only she knew the meaning of.

'Hey, what's that you're writing down, I told you it was nothing, what's she writing Paddy?'

Paddy didn't answer. He'd lost interest in the conversation, becoming slightly hypnotised watching a murmuration of starlings swooping and sweeping above the treeline, dozens of tiny bodies moving collectively, a rolling black cloud dipping and rising and turning and twisting. A kick on the shin from Monica brought his focus back to the table. 'I wonder how Pete's getting on?' he asked.

'Why'd you ask that?'

'I don't know, maybe it was the birds up there,' he responded. 'I must have made the mental connection: remember how he was worried all the birds would go and never come back? Seems he overreacted, because look at them all.'

'My colleague spoke to a Peter Brooks yesterday,' DC Sharma informed him. 'Is that who you mean?'

Paddy nodded, but again wasn't listening too closely; the birds had distracted him once more. 'I almost didn't recognise Pete yesterday, did you Mon? He looked different out of his camouflage, in normal clothes.'

'I don't expect he wears his camouflage every single day, Paddy,' replied Monica.

'He was wearing it when we were all here having a tea. But then he'd got changed when he came by to pick something up.'

'Well, maybe he was going somewhere.'

'Maybe,' agreed Paddy. 'Anyway ...'

'Anyway ...' replied Monica.

'Anyway,' added DC Sharma, 'Have you got anything else you think may be helpful? No matter how small or insignificant, you never know.'

CHAPTER **EIGHT**

'YOU'VE GOT THIS, YOU CAN DO THIS, COME ON MAN,' Edward Canning urged the face in the mirror. *Edward,* he pondered, *is that a good name for a cop?* His mind flicked through all his influences: *Life On Mars, The Professionals, The Sweeney* – Jack Regan, now there was a proper copper, that's what he aspired to, what he signed up for. To be honest he'd expected a lot more high-speed chases and 'Put your trousers on, you're nicked' and a lot less forms to fill in. He'd done twenty years of paper-pushing at the building society, now it was time for some action. *Eddie, that sounds good: the name's Canning, Eddie Canning. No. Wait. Ted! Yes, that's it. Ted. Call me DI Ted Canning.* He liked the nostalgia the name evoked: old-school coppers with leather jackets and Ford Cortinas, the *Daily Star*, roll-up fags and smoke-filled pubs. *Send for Ted Canning, the hammer of the Force.* Yes, he liked that. A message alert on his phone jerked Ted from his fantasy: newsflash, one of the industry's leading providers had offered a special reduced first-time buyer discount, zero point four five percent cheaper than anyone else; *that's a very good deal,* mulled Edward.

He gave his reflection a final once-over: shirt top button undone and tie knot flying low, raincoat collar turned up, two days' stubble nicely shading his jaw. His fingers ran across his scalp giving his hair a final mussing. He was in character: *time to nick bad guys.*

It was just a short walk along the corridor, from the Gents to the Incident Room, but with every step taken his thin veneer of confidence dissolved layer by layer. He paused outside the door, his hand resting on the push plate, and peered through the door's glazed panel. Nine or ten folks were assembled, forming a semi-circle with mismatched chairs taken from under desks throughout the room, all facing the large whiteboard that dominated most of the back wall. The whiteboard was decorated with photographs, notes and handwriting. In front of it prowled a young, athletic, confident woman. Her authority and control over the audience was evident even when viewed at this distance. With no sound travelling past the closed doors, just her posture, her demeanour, the way she gestured and used her hands when directing the attendees' attention to a section of the whiteboard display, it all showed she had high status amongst her peers, she was someone they respected and they trusted. Detective Constable Nicci Sharma, for it was she, pointed towards an aerial photograph of the Riverside Conservation Park and looked out at her colleagues. Her gaze travelled further, distracted by movement on the edge of her vision, out over their heads to the double doors at the back. Her eyes locked on to those of DI Canning peering back at her. Eye contact engaged. Simultaneously and as one, two hearts sunk in despair and despondency.

Oh no, really? she thought.

Oh no, really? he thought.

WHERE NICCI SHARMA was sore at being overlooked in favour of Canning by the upper ranks, Canning was sore at being undermined in favour of Sharma by the lower ranks. There had been times he'd considered making a formal complaint about her, but then sanity prevailed: *please sir, I wish to complain, she's more popular than me*. He'd be laughed out of the building and he knew it, so he kept it to himself and the resentment festered like a boil. However, the trouble with boils is they need lancing otherwise they have a tendency to explode and get messy, and Canning's was a ticking time bomb.

The assembly noticed the interruption in DC Sharma's delivery and began to turn, seeking the cause of her distraction. Before too long the entire room was facing him, and he couldn't mistake the disappointment and annoyance they transmitted to him in their expressions. He was self-aware enough to see that, but not enough to realise he was blaming DC Sharma for their attitudes when so far she hadn't even given any visible reaction to his presence, much less said anything. Nonetheless he held her personally responsible for undermining his authority. *Tick tick tick*, counted down his resentment bomb.

The faces lingered on him, every one of them expectant. A clammy flop sweat dampened his palms. His shirt stuck to his back. He knew what they wanted, they wanted a leader who could lead, an Alpha. Taking a deep breath he summoned the spirit of Gene Hunt and with a firm shove threw both doors open with a loud clatter: showtime!

'Right, listen up people,' he bellowed from the back of the room. 'There's been a murder. And I don't like murders on my patch, understand?'

He swaggered his way to the whiteboard, the faces of the seated turning in synchronicity to the swish of his coat tail. He surveyed the assembled team; some faces he recognised, some he didn't – including Caffrey, the young uniformed constable with the short ginger curls and inflamed skin. He was deeply engrossed in a whispered conversation with Perkins, the heavyset old malingerer beside him.

'Something to say, lad?' asked Canning. 'Come on, share it with the group.'

'It's nothing, sir,' replied the young man, 'I was just asking—'

'Then you ask me, constable. So, spit it out, what is it?'

'It's just ... what's your allotment got to do with Boot Camp Dan?'

'Is that meant to be some sort of joke, constable?'

'No sir. But—' Caffrey glowed salmon pink, he didn't like being the centre of attention, 'you said you didn't want any murders on your vegetable patch.'

Perkins swiftly covered his mouth to hide the sniggering, but it was a pointless exercise; the sound of chortling came from all corners of the room.

'My *patch*, I said my *patch*,' replied Canning in a tone he hoped conveyed power and dominance; he needed to get the respect of the room back, but young Caffrey looked blank, the word meaningless to him.

Nicci Sharma turned and spoke directly to the confused young man: 'What the DI means, is that the murder occurred in our operational region, so we've been assigned as the local squad, and he is keen that we make an arrest before anyone else gets hurt. Okay?'

Caffrey nodded, satisfied; it all made perfect sense now. 'Thanks, boss,' he replied to her.

Canning seethed at another undermining; he spoke in a quick and direct manner, determined to re-establish authority: 'So, what do we know?'

Detective Constable Sharma stepped forward. 'Boot Camp Dan, personal trainer, this was to be his big product launch,' and so she continued, repeating everything she'd already told the team in the fifteen minutes waiting for Canning to arrive.

'So, let me list the suspects, as I see them,' began Canning.

This'll be good, thought Sharma.

Canning picked up a red pen and began to write, barking names at the same time. 'Number one, Surjit Patel, camera operator. He admitted he never liked the victim and that he found him mean and tight-fisted. Patel had full access-all-areas, including backstage—'

'Actually, sir,' a voice piped up from the audience. Canning traced it to a raised hand, belonging to a young woman with glasses clutching a tablet device. She glanced at the screen then spoke. 'The forensic preliminary report surmises he'd been dead for less than an hour and given that he was broadcasting live at ten a.m. it's fair to say he was murdered between ten and half past. Surjit Patel was visible front of stage throughout that time with multiple witnesses and video footage.' The young woman withered a little under his glare. 'It's all in this morning's email from the lab, sir.'

Inside his head Canning unleashed a volley of colourful and medieval profanity. The thing about this job, he concluded, was too many emails: *how am I expected to read them all, if I spent all day wading through them, I'd get nothing done.*

'Surjit Patel stays on the list, until I say otherwise.'

Behind him he heard the rasp of nib on paper, and a smile twitched at the edges of his mouth, they were following his orders. His pen swept across the board, 'Number two, James Doyle—'

'The business partner?' Nicci Sharma was unable to keep the surprise out of her voice.

'The business partner,' confirmed Canning.

'But why? He'd invested a small fortune in the Boot Camp Dan brand, what possible motive could he have?'

'That,' this time it was Canning who was unable to keep the emotion from their voice, 'is your job to find out. Understand, Detective Constable?'

'Understood, sir.' Acid seeped from the emphasis placed on the last word.

'Number three, Monica Minton. She had an altercation with the victim, it embarrassed him on live TV and caused his big launch to be delayed, so check her out. Which brings me on to number four, her brother Paddy Minton—'

Nicci Sharma couldn't restrain herself, 'No way. Are you mad?'

'Detective Constable Sharma, you will watch your tone or I will have you removed from this investigation,' responded Canning, unsure whether he had the authority to carry out such a threat but he'd heard them say it on *Prime Suspect* and he liked the sound of it. It seemed to have worked as she sat down and stared at the floor, sulking.

'As I was saying, Paddy Minton. There's obviously bad blood between him and Boot Camp Dan, as there was with all the dogwalkers using the park, but Mr Minton is the only person in police interview that described him as their – and I quote – arch-enemy. And as far as I'm concerned that's a massive big flag.'

And as far as I'm concerned you're a massive big jerk, thought Nicci Sharma, watching the aforesaid massive big jerk preen and posture in front of the whiteboards. He was wrong though, she wasn't sulking, she was plotting. After his very public humiliation of her she'd considered consulting her union rep, there'd been plenty of witnesses to it, but she decided against it. It'd involve putting colleagues on the spot, asking them to take a side, and it seemed unfair to drag them into her personal grievance. Then she thought about having a quiet word with the BAME diversity rep, she had quite a good relationship with her, but decided against it. She knew exactly how the haters would spin it: *female, ethnic background, can't get her own way so plays the victim and blames everyone else.* She'd seen it happen to others in the past, and it was vile, she didn't want that. *Therefore*, she concluded, *I have just the one option available: I put up and shut up. From this moment forth*, she decided, *I will do exactly as DI* Law-and-Order *Canning instructs, to the letter. I will keep meticulous notes and I will file every email and log every phone call. Then when it all goes horribly wrong, which it will, I can present it all to the tribunal clearing me and hanging him out to dry. If those are your suspects, sir, and those are your instructions, then that is the path I shall follow.*

With tasks assigned, the team talk broke up. Chairs were returned to desks, bums filled them and activity began to buzz in the room. Canning surveyed the space, satisfied with his performance: *they all look busy, they all seem to respect my authority*. Sharma was back at her desk, her computer screen bright and awake, and she appeared engrossed. He awarded himself a moment to bask in self-congratulation: *I've even tamed that one, she knows her place.*

'I'M WHAT ... suspect number one? For murder? Are you insane?'

'Two things, Paddy, you're actually number four, and it's not my list it's Canning's?'

'Oh well, in that case that's all okay then. Come on Nicci, seriously, is he out of his mind?'

Nicci Sharma paused, gathering her thoughts; she'd thought about it long and hard all night, she'd lost sleep over it, but waking this morning she knew it was the right thing to do. And after her moment of reflection, she remained convinced: she should forewarn Paddy.

The car bonnet made a surprisingly comfortable seat, and the smooth metalwork radiated a soothing warmth through her thighs. She'd been waiting some time for Paddy to show but there'd been too much traipsing around that damned park this week and she was in no mood to go hunting high and low yet again for him. Instead she waited at her car for him to return, busying herself with emails on her phone and pecking at a packet of potato chips she'd picked up as part of her healthy eating spree: they claimed to be fat-free and high in protein, but they tasted of powdery cardboard and left a dry taste in her mouth. She heard her name called and looked up. Seeing Paddy approach, his face glowing from the morning's brisk exercise and his hair naturally windswept by the light breeze, Nicci welcomed the same tingle shivering through her veins that she felt at school. Guilt made a brief appearance; it tumbled through her stomach, an especially unpleasant sensation after he'd greeted her with such a warm reception. Nicci Sharma was a professional though, she was used to having the difficult conversations. She got straight to it without prevarication. Needless to say, Paddy wasn't impressed.

Nicci's experience and training told her to suspect everyone and challenge everything, but at the same time she prided herself on being a good judge of character: her judgement told her Paddy had the clarity to see this wasn't a personal attack; it wasn't her call but came from above.

'So, who are gold, silver and bronze?' asked Paddy. 'Can you tell me?'

'I probably shouldn't tell you this, but the media studies student who operated the camera was Canning's lead suspect,' replied Nicci, 'simply by being the nearest person to the body when it was discovered.'

'Sounds a bit of a stretch, if you want my opinion.'

'I don't, but nonetheless he's already been eliminated from our enquiries. He's got witnesses galore, that lad, so don't worry about him. It's you that you should be worried about.'

Paddy gave a non-committal shrug and murmur. As one of life's blessed few, he'd breezed through without hardship or hostility, struggle or suffering. Paddy had been bestowed with charm, charisma, a handsome face and far more good luck than any person truly deserves. Whilst his response may have sounded flippant and unconcerned, the truth was Paddy had never needed to worry about a thing in his life and probably didn't know how to now. Not wanting to embark on a new emotional state after lasting so long without it, Paddy simply rejected it and dealt with it in the same way as he dealt with everything else problematic: *if I don't worry about it, it won't worry about me; if I ignore it, it'll go away.*

Detective Constable Sharma had seen enough moody, brooding men pass through her interview room to tell the difference between those feigning indifference as a show of defiance, and those in ignorant denial of their predicament. Instinct and experience kicked in; she could see Paddy was squarely in the latter camp.

'Paddy, listen to me, Canning is desperate to make a quick arrest on this, and he doesn't care who. The man's an idiot, we all know it, but he wants a result to impress the top brass who also know he's an idiot. You need to have a good, solid account for your movements because the slightest quibble in your alibi and he'll use it to crucify you. Listen to me, I've seen his sort before. He doesn't know what he's doing and that makes him dangerous. What's your alibi? Run through it with me, think of it as a road test, I'll kick the tyres and check the steering, make sure it's solid and reliable.'

'But,' began Paddy, 'I don't really have one.'

'You must have. Tell me, what were you doing, who were you with?'

Paddy tried retracing his movements but was knocked offtrack when a thought occurred to him. 'Who else is on the list? If Camera Boy was number one and I'm number four, who's two and three?'

Nicci Sharma considered the question. Part of her knew she shouldn't be discussing aspects of the case such as that but another part knew – and knew from experience, it must be said – that sometimes letting go of little snippets can be enough to unlock lips and set suspects off against one another.

'James Doyle is number two,' she replied, 'but we've not been able to speak with him yet.'

Paddy seethed. He hated the idea of being beaten at anything by the Handsome Smoothie – it didn't matter that the winner got a life sentence, it was the fact that he came above him that grated.

'And number three?'

'Your sister, Monica.'

'What?' Paddy felt a lifetime's sibling rivalry flash past him; everything little thing they did, no matter what, was treated like a competition. If he'd seethed at James Doyle, the thought of Monica besting him was incendiary.

Nicci mistook his competitive outrage for defensive anger. 'She needs to be careful too. Canning's seen the video of her and Boot Camp Dan arguing. It doesn't look good for her, you need to let her know she needs a waterproof alibi before we speak with her.'

'You can tell herself if you like. In fact, tell them both if you want. They're in there.' Paddy jabbed a thumb in the direction of the Visitors' Centre. 'Monica's meeting James Doyle right now.'

CHAPTER **NINE**

SENSING THE MIGRAINE FAST APPROACHING, Monica pushed the laptop away from her. A glimpse of the clock in the bottom corner told her she'd been staring into her screen for six solid hours: building a website, drafting advertising flyers, composing newsletters and bolting together strategies for *We Sit Pets*. She needed help, and she knew who to ask: *and why not, after all didn't he say he'd welcome a chat with me?* James Doyle, by nature a man of impeccable manners, hadn't really welcomed a chat, it was actually only something said out of politeness on the spur of the moment and needless to say, he was somewhat surprised to receive Monica's night-time call, arriving out of the blue.

'Monica Minton,' she repeated, answering his belligerent question. 'When we met, I said I was an entrepreneur, you said we should talk.'

'Ah yes, that's right. Remind me, was that before or after you invaded our stage and told my investment to stick his Lycra leotard right up his—'

'Before,' answered Monica, 'and I'm sorry about that.'

'Which bit? The invasion or the altercation?'

'The invasion, it was an accident, my dog got loose. I'm not sorry for what I said.' She paused, and held it a beat too long, which somehow convinced James she was sincere when she continued, 'Actually I am. That wasn't me, I'm not normally like that, I was just so angry. If I could apologise, I would.'

James Doyle laughed; it was loud and hearty. 'To be honest, it was quite funny. You've got a very vivid imagination and a colourful turn of phrase. So, what can I do for you?'

The relief washed through Monica, and she began to speak quickly in a fast gabble: 'I'm an entrepreneur, a new business creator, I've just started out but I've got loads of ideas and lots of experience, but I'd love to get your advice and tips as what I see is that with positive growth—'

James found the rapid-fire chatter too much for him so late in the evening, and cut in, 'I'll tell you what, I need to be at the Park tomorrow morning to hand the stage back to the hire company, so how about I meet you in the Visitors' Centre? Nine thirty?'

Monica rapidly thanked him profusely, then checked herself and, rather too late, attempted to play it cool. 'Sure, I can do that. I'll see you there.'

James cut the call; in the pokey corner of her kitchen that doubled as her office Monica squealed in happy delight until Paddy called out from the other room, 'Keep it down, I'm trying to watch the Chelsea game.'

THE VISITORS' CENTRE WAS a large bright space. It felt nice; the ceiling high with hefty oak timbers, the floor laid with aged grey slate. A photo gallery showing the wildlife and local fauna in poster-sized prints lined one wall to inform and educate the visiting school parties. Along the opposite wall, near the corner, three timber beams formed an opening to the café. The beams, two uprights and a crossbar, were hewn from a mighty oak that was already ancient when Shakespeare was on his first draft. The aged and exposed timber radiated a welcoming golden glow.

The café was small and cosy with a neat, rustic look. A serving counter ran the length of the rear wall; glass cabinets displaying baked goods sat atop and a range of shiny chrome machinery stood behind. The chrome, normally a whirring, grinding, whooshing factory of coffee production, sat idle due to there being no clientele to serve. A large young woman in an apron busied herself going from empty table to empty table wiping them down and readying them for the day's custom. She straightened up to look at the incoming smartly dressed young woman. It was nine twenty-five.

Monica, in her favourite business suit and most expensive heels, perused the empty café before selecting a table towards the back corner, then deciding it wasn't right, moved to one in the opposite corner, beside the window overlooking the river. She unloaded her bag, flipped open her laptop and prepared herself for the meeting ahead.

'Could I have a cappuccino please?' she called out to the woman in the apron. The woman didn't look up from the table she was setting. She gave a grunt, the meaning of which Monica didn't know but thought it best not to follow up.

On the exact stroke of half-nine James Doyle, the Handsome Smoothie, entered the café. The woman in the apron was suddenly attentive: 'Morning, James. Cappuccino?'

'Yes please, Alison, that'd be lovely.'

Standing framed by the doorway, the aged and exposed timber radiated a golden glow around him. He was charm personified. 'And one for you too, Monica?'

Monica gratefully accepted; the woman flicked her eyes up and down Monica with suspicion then began pulling levers and pressing buttons behind the counter, filling the quiet morning with whirrs and whooshes.

James approached the table. Monica stood. She extended a straight arm then immediately cringed internally at her rigid formality. James seemingly didn't notice; with a warm smile and keeping eye contact, he clasped her hand for a short, confident shake. She introduced herself and thanked him for attending, and again immediately cringed again: *relax, Monica, come on, you've got this, just relax,* her inner voice told her.

Sitting face-to-face across the table, she got the measure of him: he looked a little older than her, mid-thirties possibly, and was tall and slim, in a gym-toned way. She liked his dress sense; he dressed like a grown-up should, not the shabby man-child T-shirts Paddy always wore. Today James looked smart but casual in a green tweed blazer, a striped business shirt open at the button-down collar, no tie, and blue jeans as dark as Indian ink; none of it had any logos but she could tell it was all good quality, expensive brands. He wore his soft brown hair in a short, fashionable style appropriate to his age. Monica approved, and rapidly tried to think of something to say to open the conversation. She eventually mustered, 'So James, do you live nearby?' and something inside her shrivelled at the corniness of it.

'Not far,' he replied. She nodded and filed that nugget of information away: *good, not too far, long-distance relationships never work.*

What? Relationships? What are you talking about? screamed her inner voice, shocked and astounded to discover her thinking this way.

Monica sat up straight and cleared her throat; outwardly she tried to project professionalism, whilst inwardly she was in a frenzy trying to shoo away those unexpected thoughts. Monica was by no means an unattractive young woman – how could she be when she shared the same genes as Paddy? However, where Paddy radiated warmth and welcome and an easy-going charisma, Monica projected anxiety, awkwardness and ambition. She'd had boyfriends in the past, a few serious but nothing that you'd call long-term. Work and making it at IGR Financial had always been the number one priority, but without that where did it leave her? All these thoughts were ruminated on at length later when alone, but for now she was flustered by the Handsome Smoothie in front of her and she struggled to get her meeting back on track. She noticed James looking closely at her, tilting his head slightly, confusing her even more.

'Wait, I know you,' he said, 'don't you work for IGR Financial? In Martin Hubbard's team?'

Monica, for reasons she couldn't quite understand, felt a chill run through her veins.

'I did,' she replied, 'but not anymore, I left last week,' and at that moment she realised the cause of the chill: this was the first time – outside of Paddy who didn't count – she'd had to admit leaving a coveted role with a prestigious employer.

'Don't blame you,' he said with a laugh in his voice. 'Bloody awful place, I got out of there five years ago. Best decision I ever made. Bet you think so too?'

The chill melted away. Monica could almost feel it rise off of her like steam; this was exactly what she needed to hear.

'What was that nonsense they used to drum into everyone at the staff conferences? *Only the best are good enough for IGR, if you can't cut it you aren't good enough.* What a load of rubbish!'

And that too!

A coffee was placed gently in front of James. 'Thanks Alison,' said James. He got a smile in return, Monica didn't. Instead, a cup landed in front of her with a surly clatter.

'First name terms?' quipped Monica, after their server had taken their bad attitude and stomped off with it.

'Boot Camp Dan had an arrangement with the manager,' replied James. 'He used the disabled toilet as his own personal changing room, and he'd meet his clients here in the café. So, this is where I'd meet with him too. I've become quite the regular over the past few months.'

Monica knew this was an opportunity for her to be taken as a serious business professional; she felt compelled to say something but she didn't know what. Eventually, for want of anything better, she found herself asking, 'Think you can get the deal back on?'

'God, no. Boot Camp Dan was the brand, it died with him,' replied James. 'But I've spent years cultivating my portfolio of investors. They're serious money, one chap in particular; where he leads everyone follows. I need to get on my knees before him and beg forgiveness if I ever want to work with him or any of them again. I need to get myself face-to-face and plead for his confidence if I'm to salvage anything from this fiasco. That's why I've booked myself on this afternoon's flight to Geneva.'

Finally, Monica's commercial brain switched on, she spotted the conversational opening and grabbed it: 'Perhaps I may be able to help you out in that case. Let me tell you about my firm. It's very new, you won't have heard of us.'

'Us?'

'Yes, it's my firm, I founded it but I've got—' below the table her fingers did a quick head-count: *me, Paddy, Hazel, Kenton and Comedy Tim*, 'Five staff, and,' her fingers fluttered again, this time a tail-count, 'seventeen clients that we're providing an exclusive personal service. That's currently, but we're looking to grow that significantly.'

James eyes widened. 'I'm impressed. You've grown that yourself from nothing? In a week?'

Monica confirmed she had and hoped her tone didn't give away the fact that less than two days ago it was just her helping out her brother until she happened upon a bunch of dreamers too lazy to do their own paperwork.

'So, I guess we're here because you want to give me all the details,' he replied. 'A business with such a rapid growth as that has clearly found a gap in the market. We could work together, make it big. What's the business called?'

'*We Sit Pets*,' Monica replied feeling foolish.

'*We Sit Pets*,' boomed James, 'I love it.'

AND SO, FOR THE next twenty-five minutes, Monica ran through her proposals and aspirations for *We Sit Pets*: a plethora of colourful graphs and diagrams were shared and explained. Monica was in her element, in her mind's eye she could picture it: *We Sit Pets* franchised across the country, an army of dogwalkers in branded hi-viz tunics in every park up and down the land, fleets of liveried vans in streets everywhere feeding cats and kittens, posters in veterinary surgeries of her holding a tin – *'the only food recommended by Monica Minton, CEO, We Sit Pets'*. The possibilities were endless. The growth limitless. *We Sit Pets* was set for the big time.

James, the Handsome Smoothie, listened intently. He'd spotted some weaknesses in her strategy, but on the whole was impressed by her passion and vision. He explained, whilst effortlessly remaining modest and charming, that exploiting the digital world was his greatest talent.

'Your website is pretty good for a first attempt, and the idea of a weekly newsletter to subscribers is a good idea,' he said, 'but that's strictly one-way traffic. It's you telling the world about *We Sit Pets*. To give yourself the advantage, you need to discover what the public are saying about you. That way you can react instantly and adapt, before it's too late.' He pointed at the laptop, open on the table. 'May I?'

Monica gave her agreement and he swivelled it to face him. His fingers danced across the keys: *tip tap tip tap*. A few minutes later, he turned it back to the middle so they could both see the screen.

'I've downloaded my own program, and I've set the search terms to *Monica Minton* and *We Sit Pets*. It'll run in the background every minute of the day. As soon as anything is posted on the internet, anywhere in the world, any time day or night, that mentions either your name or the business, you'll get an update and a link to it. It's active right now.' As if on cue, the laptop chimed. 'There you go, your first notification, why don't you take a look?'

Monica followed James's instructions, and opened the program then clicked the link it offered. A news site opened up, with an article about Boot Camp Dan's demise. Monica skim-read it quickly; near the bottom she spotted her name.

'Oh look, there I am.' She proceeded to read aloud the relevant paragraph: '*The live launch had been three months in the planning. Over twelve thousand subscribers had logged in to watch the event in real time, but they were disappointed to see instead Boot Camp Dan become embroiled in a hot-tempered dispute and altercation with Ms Monica Minton, the director of We Sit Pets. The live launch was subsequently postponed, at which point Boot Camp Dan was found dead.*'

She stopped reading. Then re-read it, this time silently to herself.

'Oh. I wish I hadn't seen that now. It doesn't make me sound very nice.'

'I wouldn't worry about it—'

But before James Doyle, the business guru, could explain why not to worry, the laptop chimed another notification, then again, and again, and again, and again, and again.

'What's happening, James?'

James clicked through on the links, opening up an internet forum page. He gave a satisfied sounding 'uh-huh', then informed Monica, 'I've been here before, many times. It's a message board for Boot Camp Dan fans. They all gather here and post their comments. He attracted quite a following, they call themselves Das Booties, it's quite sweet really.'

'Not today it's not,' replied Monica. 'Look at this one: *"Monica Minton, what a bitch!"* Charming.'

She scrolled through the comments. Every single one of them was angry and vitriolic: *"Monica Minton ruined Boot Camp Dan ... Who does Monica Minton think she is threatening our Dan ... Does anyone else think Monica Minton killed Dan ... I do, she definitely killed our BCD ... Monica Minton should hang ... Justice for BCD ..."*

'Oh my god, this is horrible,' said Monica. The laptop pinged more notifications; more and more messages were being added. 'They're accusing me. They hate me. They don't even know me.'

'Please, don't worry about it,' replied James. 'As I was about to say, any mention is a good mention, trust me, it means you're being talked about.'

'But they're being horrible about me.'

'Doesn't matter.' his voice was smooth, soft and reassuring. 'The algorithm doesn't care, all it cares about is the mention. The more mentions you get the higher priority your website gets in any searches. The higher the priority, the more advertising revenue. Believe me, any mention is a good mention.'

'But—'

'Don't worry about the comments. They're all sad lonely women getting protective over their fantasy man. It's all chit-chat, but nothing will come of it and they'll have got it out of their system in a day or two.'

Monica felt reassured, tension began to dissipate and her nerves relaxed: *this is his specialist area after all and his manner's so comforting, he clearly knows what he's talking about. I'm sure everything will be fine.*

'Now then,' James leaned forwards, resting on his elbows, 'when I mentioned going to Geneva, you said you could help me out. Tell me how.'

'Ah yes,' replied Monica, remembering. 'If you're away for the next few days, is there anyone special at home we could look after for you? Think of it as a trial run. If we impress you, you will see for yourself how good a prospect *We Sit Pets* could be.'

'You mean we treat this as the dress rehearsal to the big time?' laughed James, the Handsome Smoothie. He paused, as if in thought, then said, 'Actually, Uncle Albert will need looking after while I'm away.'

'Ah, no, sorry, there must've been some confusion,' stammered Monica, 'we don't do that kind of home care. Doesn't he have any relatives who can care for him?'

'Relatives?'

Then, in a gesture to mask his embarrassment he cleared his throat; he continued with an apologetic tone, 'I'm sorry, I should have explained, Uncle Albert is the name of my cat. He's white and fluffy, like the TV character.'

'Ah, of course, I see,' Monica lied: a laser-focussed determination to forge a career meant she had very little time to watch television and had fallen out of the habit a very long time ago. '*We Sit Pets* does cats. I'd love to look after him for you.'

'Great, then it's all sorted then,' replied James. He proceeded to give her the details of the cat's dietary requirements and feeding times. Monica murmured affirmations at the right time, but most of it passed across her consciousness like white noise. Her mind was elsewhere: she still couldn't shake the bad-tempered messages, and knew that when she next opened her laptop there'd be plenty more waiting for her.

Nonetheless James waffled on about his beloved cat's regime, until a word triggered an alarm inside her, dragging her away from her own thoughts with a warning that she needed to pay attention: 'What was that, James?'

With a little poke of his finger to indicate the back of the room behind her, he replied, 'I said, it appears someone wants to join our meeting.'

Monica twisted in her seat and discovered standing only a few feet from her, with arms crossed in sullen displeasure, DC Nicci Sharma.

'If you've quite finished your cosy little chat, perhaps you wouldn't mind helping me with my enquiries.'

CHAPTER 10

FEELING THE SHAME BURN HIS CHEEKS, PADDY APOLOGISED. 'Sorry, Mon. It was me, I mentioned you were in here.'

Paddy had been left dumbfounded: *all I did was mention they were in the Visitors' Centre and she stormed the place.*

Sensing he was in trouble with Nicci Sharma and anticipating he'd be in trouble with Monica, he dashed after the detective, arriving seconds behind her. In an attempt to show sibling solidarity, he took a seat at the table beside Monica.

Nicci Sharma didn't seem to mind, in fact it made her life simpler: she could deal with them all together at once. Wishing to maintain a degree of separation, she took a seat on the table across the aisle and removed the digital recorder and notebook from her pocket; time to get down to it.

Paddy interrupted her train of thought: 'Looks like you've got company.'

A police car had pulled up outside. All present reacted to Paddy's prompt, and turned to see two uniformed officers getting out of the car. The male driver put on his hat and slammed the door harder than necessary.

'What do they want?' Nicci Sharma pondered aloud, already having a reasonable idea but not wanting to be proven right.

The passenger, a female police officer, saw them all staring at her. She tilted her head, almost dropping her ear to her shoulder. She gave them a perfect u-shaped smile and tiny wiggle of the fingers as a wave of greeting; if it hadn't been for the uniform, you'd have thought her a nursery school worker.

THERE ARE TWO police officers guarding me: Monica couldn't quite believe how her life had changed in less than a week. Last Thursday she was at a strategy meeting planning to outsource a major insurer's call-centre operations from the UK to Asia, this Thursday: *'There are two police officers guarding me.'*

The female one was small, rotund and young. Her uniform sat cumbersome on her, bulking her up even more. It made her almost spherical, and her legs looked short and skinny; they poked out beneath her like a sparrow's. The male officer wasn't tall and had a head too big for his shoulders. He had eyes that bulged and didn't seem to blink; Monica didn't like the way he cast them around the room, assessing and cataloguing everything he saw.

As soon as they arrived the male went across to Nicci Sharma and leaned his head close to hers. A murmur of one-sided conversation could be heard, but not clearly enough to hear what was actually said. Fury erupted across Nicci Sharma's face. She stormed out. The male officer looked across to his female partner and said, 'Ten minutes.'

The female spoke: 'Miss Minton, can I call you Monica?' Monica knew she would regardless, whether she liked it or not, and gave a resigned shrug of consent. 'Monica, my name is Constable Slater, and this is my colleague Constable Harvey.'

Harvey stared at Monica. Monica stared back.

'Now then,' Slater spoke with a soft comforting voice, 'let's have a little shuffle about, so Monica, you stay where you are, and gents, if one of you could go over there, and the other over there. Good, that's it. Thank you.'

Slater slid into the seat vacated by James, opposite Monica, without invitation and sat wordlessly. Harvey, the male officer with the bulging peepers, stood leaning against the wall, midway between the two men: Paddy and James were dispatched to opposite ends of the room.

FIVE MINUTES HAD PASSED. Nobody had spoken. Monica looked over at Slater; she responded by leaning forwards, her elbows on the table. Curled over she resembled a small bird more than ever. As she leaned ever closer Monica half expected to be pecked at, but instead, in that soft comforting voice more suitable for a nursery school: 'Please be patient, just another five minutes.'

Even without looking at Paddy in the opposite corner to her, Monica knew he didn't like this situation either. She could sense his antagonised state, almost as if it was a physical force, a form of static pricking her arms and making her neck tingle. She hoped Paddy could keep a lid on his temper. She didn't want them finding any reason to stay longer.

Outside the window Nicci Sharma strode back and forth, her phone pressed against her ear; her body language made it clear it wasn't a social call.

AN AWKWARD ELEVEN minutes later:

The small man in the beige raincoat entered the room with long strides, as though he was in a hurry to get somewhere. With a flick he brandished a warrant card in Monica's face, too close for her to focus and too fast for her to read. A snap of the wrist and it was back in his jacket pocket.

He turned his back to the room and feigned an interest in a child's artwork print on the wall. 'I'm Detective Inspector Canning,' he said to the wall. Canning had seen Columbo do it and thought it a nifty move, setting him up with an air of superiority. He believed it gave the impression the detective is putting every tiny aspect of life under the microscope, no matter how trivial or mundane. If he'd turned, he'd have seen Paddy's face of disgusted incredulity pulled for Monica. Slater saw it and stifled back a snigger, skilfully disguising it as a small sneeze.

'I've been trying to contact you all morning. Would you care to explain why you've been ignoring my calls, Miss Minton?'

Monica sat up in surprise. She reached for her phone: five missed calls. 'Silent mode. I've been in a meeting, I'm afraid,' she explained, and across the room James Doyle the Handsome Smoothie gallantly offered confirmation. Paddy gave him a sideways look that said, 'There's something about you, Handsome Smoothie, that I don't trust.'

'I take it from your contribution, Mr Doyle, that you too were involved with this meeting, which is why you also ignored my calls?'

Canning was ruffled, but he was satisfied no-one had noticed. They had. Everyone had. 'And what's your excuse, Mr Minton, why didn't you answer my calls?'

'I don't answer numbers I don't recognise. I can't be doing with cold callers,' replied Paddy. Slater gave a nod of understanding. 'If it's important, I figure they'll call back.'

'I *did* call back,' Canning's explosive stress on the word *did* showed his frustration, 'I called back three times.'

'Oh, I must've recognised the number after all,' replied Paddy. Slater wasn't quick enough to hide her snigger this time. Canning's mind whirred, trying to decipher Paddy's response.

It was fortunate for Paddy that Monica stepped in before he'd worked it out, and distracted him. 'Well, we're all here now. What do you want?'

'You two,' Canning used both hands to point at Monica and Paddy in opposite corners of the room, 'There's something about you I don't like.'

'Yeah, well the feeling's—'

'Paddy,' Monica cautioned her brother. 'Mr Canning, I don't appreciate your tone. If you want to speak with my brother and me, please be civil otherwise we will ask for our solicitor to be present.'

Nobody responded like that on the TV. *That's the problem with this country,* thought Canning, *everyone knowing their rights.* Canning took a pause, then began again: 'I would like to speak to you both. We can do it here, or at the station, your choice.'

'Thank you, here's fine,' replied Monica.

Canning thrust his fists in his pockets and stuck out his chest. 'I'd been looking for a killer but then it struck me over breakfast this morning. What if they come in a pair? And what comes in a pair? The Mintons!'

Paddy and Monica shared the same expression of two parts astonished one part horrified.

Paddy was the first to protest. 'Are you out of your mind?'

Monica chided her brother, wanting him to keep his volatility at bay. 'Paddy, that's enough. But seriously Mr Canning, are you out of your mind?'

'Oh no, I am far from out of my mind, I am perfectly one hundred and ten per cent serious.' The smugness ringing through Canning's voice made Slater look to her shoes in embarrassment. He hadn't finished, 'You two, where were you between ten and ten thirty on the morning Boot Camp Dan was killed?'

'Seriously? You know this already,' replied Monica, 'I told that young policeman of yours. Caffrey? Was that his name?'

'Yeah, and I told everything to Nicci.' Paddy noticed Monica stiffen at the sound of her first name. 'I mean, I told everything to DC Sharma.'

'So why are you wasting our time and asking us all over again?' demanded Monica.

Canning wanted to scream: *these people are infuriating, why won't they respect my authority?*

What would they do in *The Sweeney*? Canning summoned his best TV tough guy persona and attempted to reimpose the higher status: 'How about you tell me? And cut out the attitude.'

'Fine,' sighed Paddy, 'we were at the Munsters'.'

Monica spotted Canning's confusion and couldn't be bothered with more bad-tempered questions. 'The mobile tea-hut at the far end of the park, near the river,' she clarified.

'Any witnesses?' challenged Canning.

Paddy laughed: *he's actually laughing at me*; Canning bristled.

'Me and Monica, three other dogwalkers, Pete from the birdwatching club and Mr Munster himself, so what's that

... seven? Check your files, it's all in there, and their statements too I'd expect,' replied Paddy.

Canning's memory flipped through the case file pages, but most appeared blank on account of the scantest of skim-throughs he'd given them over his morning croissant.

'So, Mr Canning, we've proven quite easily we didn't have the opportunity,' said Monica, warming to her role as defender of the downtrodden. 'How about you share with us our motive for carrying out this crime?'

Canning knew he was on firmer ground here; the frustration left his face, replaced by a sneer. '*Arch-enemy*. Does that ring any bells?' he said directly to Paddy, and then turned to Monica. 'And as for you, close to fifteen thousand people and rising have now witnessed you going toe-to-toe with Boot Camp Dan trading insults and threats. So yeah, I think that's motives all round, don't you?'

Paddy rose, his body tense, his hands balled in fists. Monica noticed. 'Paddy, take a breath,' she said to him in a calm voice, before facing Canning. 'I think that's enough for now. If you want to talk to us any further, we'd like our solicitor present.' Monica gestured to the door with a gentle sweep of her arm, 'Now, if you'd like to go, please.'

Canning seethed. He didn't appreciate being spoken to like this in front of junior officers. However, something needled him in the back of his brain, it told him he didn't have enough to charge them ... yet.

With a raging sense of regret, and with pursed lips, he left the café without saying goodbye. Paddy flopped back down to his seat and blew out a sigh. Monica burst into tears.

CHAPTER **ELEVEN**

THE STAGE HAD GONE. LIKEWISE, THE TOWER. They served no further purpose. The police had finished with them, and Boot Camp Dan clearly wasn't coming back. The hire company had dismantled them earlier that morning, leaving barely a trace; it hadn't been there long enough to blanch the grass, just a few indentations in the soft ground that were already fading. James Doyle met with the foreman of the crew, and in his effortless charming way apologised for keeping them waiting: 'Unfortunately the police wanted a word,' he offered by way of explanation. The foreman held out a form for James to sign, then tore off the pink carbon-copy, handed it to James, hopped in his van and drove away.

James returned to Monica and Paddy. 'I need to go if I'm to catch my flight,' he said. 'You'll look after Uncle Albert?'

Monica assured him the cat would be fine and wished him a safe flight. She watched him leave. When he was safely out of earshot, she turned to her brother. 'I'm scared, Paddy. Can they really think it was us?'

'Canning's hoping if he shakes enough trees something ripe will fall at his feet.' Paddy's unusual lack of confidence was noticeable. 'Besides, remember what Nicci Sharma said: he's a useless idiot out of his depth.'

'She also said he could be dangerous. If he's hurling accusations about, we don't want them coming our way. What if someone important believes him? Maybe we should speak with a solicitor?'

Paddy replied 'No' which meant *yes, but leave me out of it.*

'Okay,' murmured Monica, which meant *leave it to me.*

THE DOGS WERE JUMPY. They pulled on their leashes, and veered across each other's lanes. The behaviour wasn't good, and in his gentle way Paddy admonished them, asking for better. They responded. For a short while. Minutes later they were pulling again. They strained to turn left.

'What's got into you guys today?' Paddy asked the pack. 'Is it because we're late out this morning? We said sorry. It wasn't our fault. It was that nasty man wasting our time.'

After some initial resistance, they began to settle and resumed their normal behaviour of a placid prowl. 'Come on, let's do the long walk, stretch our legs and get some fresh air.'

'Sounds like a good idea,' Monica approved, swapping her heels for wellies. The smell of ozone drifting in from the river and the mild warmth of the sun seemed the ideal cure to clear her head and chase out her worries. Monica, Paddy and their hounds of all varieties walked on, happy and relaxed. They didn't notice they were being watched from the park bench on the far side of the field.

'HERE THEY ARE. Where've you been? We were about to call out a search party.'

Paddy and Monica's longer walk, like all their walks, brought them to the Munsters' cabin and they were more pleased than they'd expected to be to find Hazel, Tim and Kenton there. Monica told them about their experience that morning with Canning whilst Paddy went to the hatch to order teas. By the time she'd finished telling them, Paddy was back and taking a seat at the table next to her.

'What are you going to do?' asked Hazel, sounding more curious than concerned.

'Monica suggested we – eugh, flowery,' Paddy swapped cups with Monica, 'Monica's first thought was to speak to a solicitor, but I'm not sure.' The curious faces prompted him to explain. 'Won't it look like we've got something to hide? I mean, only guilty people need lawyers, don't they?' The expressions coming back at him let him know he was quite wrong in that view.

'I'll make an appointment as soon as possible,' Monica said to assure him she'd take care of it, 'but I must admit I'm not comfortable being under the microscope. I still can't fathom why we've become public enemy number one.'

'Well, you did threaten to wrap his muscles around his—'

'In the heat of an argument,' Monica blurted. 'Anyway, he said far worse to me.'

'But he's dead and you're not,' pointed out Hazel, thinking she was helping.

'Boot Camp Dead,' added a voice, 'No, Boot Corpse Dan.' Tim thought he was funny. The silence around the table thought otherwise.

Kenton shuffled in his seat; he swung a thick muscular leg over the opposite knee, and cleared his throat. 'He was always trouble, ever since he was a young boy. Trouble all the way.'

Kenton's comment intrigued Paddy: 'Do you think that might be what got him killed? Someone from his past caught up with him?'

Kenton's massive square paddle of a hand swept across his mouth; he considered his words. 'I have no idea,' he eventually answered, 'I knew him through boxing. He was going places, even as a schoolboy you could see that. We all knew he attracted trouble but hoped he'd grow out of it. He had a talent. He seemed to be on the threshold of making it, then one day, he disappeared.'

'Disappeared?'

'Disappeared. I can't think of a better word,' insisted Kenton. 'One day he had it all ahead of him. The next, he'd gone. I've no idea where. Or why. And then about nine months ago, all these years later, he turns up again. Only, he's not The Dynamite Danny Usborne anymore, he's Boot Camp Dan.'

'I wonder what happened?' replied Paddy, with eyes that implored Kenton to tell him more. Kenton shrugged and relaxed back into his seat, his tale told.

It was at this point Hazel perked up. 'Perhaps I can help?'

All heads swivelled in her direction and watched her rummage in the backpack she'd kept on her lap. Her dogs sat up expectantly with big eyes and perked ears; they knew when Hazel opened the backpack treats and toys came their way. Their ears drooped with the disappointment of a green spiral-bound notebook being withdrawn rather than something tasty. They settled back down to doze in a shaft of sunlight.

'Et voilà,' Hazel laid her notebook on the table. 'Right, are you sitting comfortably? Shall I begin?'

'Just one question,' replied Comedy Tim. 'We're allowed in the nice café at the Visitors' Centre now, so why are we still here drinking at the Ebola Canteen?'

At the serving hatch behind him, the completely bald and spherical head furrowed his monobrow and sighed his dismay.

'Because it's a lovely day today,' replied Hazel. 'The sun's shining, the sky's clear and blue, the river's calm and flat. It's beautiful. Do you really want to be indoors on a day like today? You'd miss all of this.'

'That's true,' Monica agreed, knowing Hazel had no idea how prophetic her words may be: if she and Paddy couldn't distance themselves from Canning's suspicion, they'd be spending a lot of time indoors.

Paddy raised a finger, as if in class. 'I've a question please, Hazel. Why've you got notes on Boot Camp Dan?'

Hazel, dressed in yet another impressive outfit that would have looked knockout on Twiggy back in the day, regarded him as if addressing a particularly slow child. 'Because I'm a researcher. It's what I do. Sometimes, just to keep my hand in and my skills sharp I research someone. Anyone famous is too easy, they've all been written about at length so I usually do someone ordinary, someone I know. As he was the hot topic this week, I thought I'd do him.'

'Have you done me?' asked Paddy.

'Oh yes,' answered Hazel, 'darling, I've done all of you.'

An uncomfortable glance shuttled around the table, unsure whether Hazel was joking; an uneasy silence settled, as they became certain she wasn't. In the quiet, each one of them busily searched their conscience for their own guilty secret and wondered first of all, how much of it would be discoverable and, more importantly, how much did Hazel know?

Hazel, oblivious to the concern she'd created, opened the notebook: 'Kenton, you were absolutely right. Boot Camp Dan, previously The Dynamite Danny Usborne, was quite the athlete. By the age of fifteen he'd won belts and championships in the middleweight division at county and national level.'

Kenton, happy to be vindicated, gave a short nod and murmur in agreement.

'At nineteen,' continued Hazel, 'he was selected to represent Ireland in their Olympic squad. He was born and raised in South London but he qualified for selection via his mother, Helen, who came from Cork.'

'That's all very interesting,' Monica tried her hardest to keep on the right side of polite, 'but we already knew all this from Kenton. The detail about his mum adds a bit of colour, but ... so what?'

Hazel gave Monica the sort of wide-eyed smile that says *prepare to be dazzled*: 'I was just coming to the good part. Or bad. Depends which way you look at it I suppose. I mean—'

'Hazel?'

'Okay. So, he's nineteen years old, champion boxer, destined for Olympic glory. According to some of the articles I found he was strongly tipped to be on the medal podium, some even suggested gold was possible. And then, as we all know, if you're an Olympic medallist a life of fame and fortune awaits. The only thing is ... he never went to the Olympics.'

Paddy blinked in surprise: 'But why not? If he was so strongly tipped, why didn't he go? Did he get injured?'

'Sadly, no. Now this took a bit of research, but I got there in the end. Because it was the Ireland squad, it didn't get the attention of the English newspapers, so I needed to do a search of those published in the Republic—'

'And?'

'In the months leading up to the Olympics, Dynamite Danny Usborne failed to turn up to all of his statutory drugs tests.'

'And?'

'The Olympic squad committee issued him a final warning: comply or lose your place in the team. Meanwhile, the Metropolitan Police had been mounting undercover surveillance on a number of gyms across South East London believed to be involved in supplying performance-enhancing drugs.'

'And?'

'I'm getting to it, Paddy. Performance enhancers were found in his blood samples, he failed the statutory drug test. But not only that: they were found in his car, in his locker and in his home. Enough for the police to charge him with intent to supply. He got a prison sentence for it. Two years in Elmley prison.'

'Two years? Wow! Serious stuff then.'

'He was lucky. He could have got up to fourteen years for supplying steroids. The court reports say they took into account his previously clean criminal record and his sporting achievements. You might think him lucky getting his sentence reduced but whilst he was incarcerated, he missed both the Olympics and the following Commonwealth games. There's no record of him boxing again after being released.'

Monica and Paddy exchanged a glance. 'What are you thinking, Mon?' asked Paddy.

'It explains why he suddenly disappeared off the scene. And, giving him the benefit of the doubt that it was a youthful mistake, I guess I can understand why someone would want to reinvent themselves after an experience like that. Also, having the lifestyle of the rich and famous almost within your reach and then losing it all over a youthful mistake, I can kind of see why he was so driven and single-minded now. He was trying to make up for lost time and get back on top, ignoring whoever he trampled on to get there.'

Comedy Tim snorted a response, a mocking derisory sound, as if the mere suggestion of finding excuses for Boot Camp Dan's behaviour was laughable.

Paddy ignored him, and raised his concern. 'Does it help us though?' he asked. 'Should we take it to Nicci? Maybe she could follow it as a lead, and divert Canning and the police attention from us?'

'Truthfully, I don't know,' replied Monica. 'Was he still involved with that kind of thing? Could he have fallen out with someone from the drug trade? Who knows? We've no way of knowing, and to be honest with you it's not the sort of thing I want to find out. I think you're right Paddy, let's share this with Nicci Sharma, let her look into it. Hopefully she'll see we're trying to help.'

CHAPTER **TWELVE**

NICCI SHARMA HAD IGNITED THE FLAMETHROWER and was ready to unleash her fury. A surprise call from Paddy distracted her just in the nick of time: some people may never know how lucky they'd been.

Harvey, the bobby with the bulging eyes, whispered in her ear, 'I'm sorry Nic, we've been told by Canning to detain the suspects until he gets here. No-one's to talk to them except him. Sorry.'

Incandescent with rage, she stormed out of the Visitors' Centre and started making calls. Nobody picked up. They knew why she was calling and they wanted to stay well out of it, deep below the parapet. This was her fight with Canning and they wanted nothing to do with it. Predicting a career-ending incident was likely if still there when Canning arrived, she knew the best thing she could do was go somewhere else; anywhere.

Her bad mood had guided her nowhere in particular, and it was only when hunger pangs struck that she realised where she was: a short distance up ahead a department store, a stalwart of the High Street, dominated the corner. The lure of warm, safe nostalgia was too great. Nicci pushed open the grand brass door and rode the escalator upwards, driven by fond memories of Saturday mornings spent with Mum and Auntie Reeta enjoying tea and cake in the top floor restaurant after browsing the fashions.

THE TOP FLOOR RESTAURANT had been refurbished since the childhood shopping trips she remembered so fondly. It had a bright and fresh look in soft pastels with colourful modern art on the wall. She pushed the half-eaten brownie to one side, disappointed: it looked better than it tasted and wasn't worth the calories. Inside her head she considered everyone on the team, then she tried to work out who it might have been that had told Canning. He wasn't smart enough to have known by himself where she was or who with. He must've been tipped off, and that prospect made her even angrier. Inside her head, she arranged the line-up of potential suspects, got them up against the wall and sparked up the flamethrower. Then, her phone rang.

It was Paddy suggesting they meet for a drink after work. A flutter she hadn't experienced in a long while tickled through her. She proposed a popular new bar in town: it was far enough away from the police station that it wouldn't be the first place colleagues piled into at the end of a shift, and she knew it was unlikely they'd be spotted. Given her current animosity towards her co-workers, the very last thing she needed was curious questions or teasing from the regular gossipmongers next morning. Two floors down, she bought herself a new top and some cosmetics: no point going all the way home just to get changed in order to come back into town, she said to convince herself the price tag was worth it.

THE BAR OCCUPIED THE former premises of a bank on a main shopping street long since fully pedestrianised. Even so early in the evening it was busy. Filled with the after-work crowd, hordes of office workers loosened their ties around tables too close together under the exposed brick and steel industrial urban decor. Out on the pavement, a velvet rope suspended between chrome posts marked out the bar's external boundary. Several square tables and matching chairs filled the space and most were occupied. It was cool out there and people could smoke.

Nicci checked her reflection in a shop window: new dark lipstick and a bit of mascara, her new top under her work blazer, her glossy black hair released to hang loosely around her shoulders, she looked and felt amazing.

She instantly spotted Paddy on her arrival; the back of his head familiar. He was at an outside table facing the opposite direction to her. She paused, took a deep breath, brushed a stray tendril of hair from her face, and Paddy, for reasons known only to him, chose that moment to turn. He caught sight of her and waved, beckoning her to the table.

Paddy stood as she approached; ever the gentleman. Face to face, inches between them. A loud roar from the mob behind him deafened Paddy. A birthday or a leaving or a promotion, who cares, they were enjoying themselves. It was boisterous, raucous and Paddy's greeting got smothered by their noise; lost unheard. Take two: Paddy bowed at the waist and angled his face towards her cheek.

Nicci was impressed that Paddy rose to greet her, it showed manners. Around her, the volume of chatter increased; every table competed with its neighbour to be heard. Lots of young men with shiny suits and bottled lager brayed, hollered and whooped but she knew they were beginning to flag. Her years in the local constabulary told her the after-work crowd had peaked, there'd be another half-hour of this, then all but the die-hards and bachelors would disperse, sloping off home for their tea and the evening soaps. And so, the hiatus would begin: a quiet period lasting an hour and a half, two hours tops, before the night-time crowd come out for clubbing and cocktails. Nicci always liked the hiatus. It was the sweet spot for a first date: quiet enough to chat and get the measure of someone, and then when the party people began congregating you could either bail out ('*oh look at the time, it's getting late and I've a busy day tomorrow*') or you could go with the flow and join the party.

Paddy looked awkward standing waiting for her. His lips moved but she couldn't hear a word; anything spoken drowned out by the commotion all around them. She took a half-step closer and noticed him bending forwards, leaning in to her. She felt a tremor of silly excitement. She placed a hand on his shoulder and leaned in to meet him halfway. As she kissed him gently on the cheek he shouted in her ear: 'I said, do you want a drink? Monica's just gone to the bar.'

WHAT? OH MY GOD! What have I just done? What did he say? How did I get this so wrong? A blizzard of thoughts and recriminations tumbled through Nicci's head. She wanted the ground to swallow her – no – she wanted to cry: *oh my god, I actually want to cry.*

If only Nicci had known how he'd interpreted the kiss, perhaps she may have relaxed, because Paddy was a simple man of plain tastes: *that was quite sophisticated of her, very continental greeting, clearly she's a classy girl.*

Paddy's head swivelled back and forth, trying to locate Monica in the writhing mass of bodies. It was hopeless. The bar was at least three deep with punters eager for their '*one more then I've really got to go*' consolation drink; more joined every second. Paddy had an idea: *I'll text Monica.* As he thumbed his message, his mind found a new path to wander: *Nicci looks nice, there's something different about her, hair maybe, and she smells nice too, and she kissed me.* And then his mind corrected its course and was back on track; he thumbed send and hoped Monica would feel it vibrate, knowing it unlikely she'd hear it.

Monica's fingers tingled. Paddy's message had travelled a million miles into outer space then bounced straight back down again, landing on the phone in her hand, no more than twelve feet from where it began its journey. A few minutes later, Monica weaved her way back to their table clutching two glasses of dry white, and a bottle of lager for Paddy.

Nicci's police instincts proved correct; by the time they'd finished their first round of drinks the crowds had dispersed; the watcher however remained. From a few tables away they looked on; sitting a few tables away in a busy bar, hidden in plain sight, the watcher studied the Mintons.

'CAN WE GET TO why we wanted to see you?' asked Monica to Nicci, who responded with a shrug of 'why not?' – the reminisces about school were fine, but she was just as keen to get to the point.

'It's about Boot Camp Dan,' said Paddy, 'We've got something that may be of interest to you.'

Nicci sat up straight, her interest piqued. Paddy glanced to Monica, a look that handed across the conversational responsibility. Monica accepted, and in serious and formal tones conveyed to Detective Constable Sharma everything they'd learnt from Hazel that afternoon.

THE MINTON SIBLINGS stared at Nicci Sharma. Their tale told, they wanted feedback. Nicci Sharma held her palms up towards them in query: 'Is that it?'

Paddy's crestfallen face whipped a pang of guilt straight through her.

Monica, however, was confused. 'What do you mean?'

'Is that it?' repeated Nicci, 'Is that all you had to tell me?'

The Mintons looked at each other then back at her, they nodded slowly in unison.

'Boot Camp Dan's drug history? That's the first thing that came up about him the moment we opened the case. It's hardly a ground-breaking discovery.'

'Oh,' replied Monica, 'but we only found out about it today.'

'Yeah. Why didn't you tell us about it?' asked Paddy.

'Why didn't—' Nicci spluttered on her pinot grigio, 'More to the point – why would I? In case you've forgotten, you're not police. You're totally irrelevant.'

'Are we?' asked Monica. She'd spotted a tiny golden glimmer and intended to mine it. 'Inspector Canning didn't think so this morning when he bumped you out.'

'When I said irrelevant, I meant as part of the investigative team,' replied Nicci Sharma. 'You still remain people of interest.'

'Do we? Until when?' asked Paddy.

'Until that idiot Canning decides otherwise,' was Nicci's truthful answer.

'That's what we were worried about,' replied Monica. 'That's why we thought we were being helpful, by letting you see there was more to Boot Camp Dan than met the eye.'

'Yes, I understand that, and I sympathise, honestly I do. Look, between you and me: Canning is under enormous pressure about this case. Everyone can see he's miles out of his depth and doesn't know what he's doing. He's been making promises he has no way of delivering. I heard a whisper he's been told the top brass: get a result or get lost.' Nicci's voice was a conspiratorial whisper. 'If I were you, I'd answer his questions then keep my head down and stay as far away from him as possible, and hope he forgets all about you. He needs a quick result, he's an idiot and that makes him dangerous. Okay?'

Paddy and Monica resembled a pair of nodding dogs. Their heads bobbed silently up and down. They contemplated what they'd just heard; they knew it was their only option even though it was little more than close your eyes and hope it goes away.

Monica glanced at her watch, she'd had enough for one day, some quiet me-time was called for. Monica switched on her phone to access an app she had for ordering minicabs.

Ping, ping, ping, ping, ping, ping.

'Someone's popular tonight,' Paddy joked, amused by the barrage of messages hitting Monica's phone. From the sharp shake of her head and the hard set to her eyes, Paddy could tell she was in no mood for jokes. 'What is it, Mon? What's up?'

'Hate mail! Das Booties have traced me, got my email address and phone number—'

'How?'

'I suppose they've got it off the *We Sit Pets* website. Look at the vile stuff they're sending me. It's been coming all afternoon.'

Monica passed her phone to Paddy. He glanced down at the screen then straight back at her: 'Mon, this is horrendous.'

From over Paddy's shoulder, Nicci could see the screen. She too was appalled. 'Monica, this is against the law. It's threatening and abusive behaviour, it's harassment. Would you like me to deal with it?' Monica confirmed she would, and thanked her.

Nicci took the phone from Paddy. She made screenshots of all the messages then emailed them to herself. 'Leave it with me, I'll see what I can do. In the meantime, set up an autoreply saying all abusive emails will be forwarded to the police, and put a similar warning on your website; we find that usually scares them off as mostly they're gutless cowards. Don't let them get to you.'

'Thank you, Nicci,' replied Monica, rising to her feet. 'I'm going, I'll see you at home Paddy, good night.' Paddy and Nicci bid her farewell and watched her leave; neither noticed the person three tables across also get up and walk out, following not so far behind her.

'Another one?' Paddy tilted an empty glass in Nicci's direction. A broad smile signified her acceptance: *maybe this evening isn't such a washout after all*, she thought.

CHAPTER **THIRTEEN**

THE FOLLOWING DAY, on the kitchen table that acted as the nerve centre for We Sit Pets, the phone buzzed. The search was on. Monica swatted piles of loose papers, lifted notepads and patted pockets until she eventually located the errant device. Snatching it she jabbed the “accept” icon before the caller gave up or the network dropped the call. Her eagerness was motivated by the hope they were calling in response to one of the three hundred flyers she'd paid the neighbour's boy to poke through every letterbox in the area.

However, on this occasion it wasn't anyone calling in response to her flyers. To be honest, it was unlikely it would've been given how the neighbour's boy got bored after the first four houses and dumped the remaining two hundred and ninety-six in the recycling bin behind the church. And the twenty pounds she'd paid him? That was currently being spent in Nando's, impressing a hot young exchange student from his A-level German class.

'Hello, *We Sit Pets*.'

'You deserve to die for what you did to Boot Camp Dan, you—'

Monica cut the call and dropped the phone like it was radioactive. Her open-mouthed surprise resembled the current expression of the neighbour's boy who'd just swallowed half a bottle of the hottest sauce Nando's had to offer in his bid to impress the young fräulein. Needless to say, she wasn't. Funnily enough the capability to ingest hot chilli sauce in ulcer-rupturing quantities doesn't rank particularly high on what loosens a young Bavarian's lederhosen these days.

The neighbour's boy was presently unable to speak. With his throat burning, and his tongue swollen to proportions at least three times too big for his mouth, he frantically, wordlessly, sought ice cubes, and plenty of them, to suck hoping it would loosen up his scorched vocal chords. If she'd known, Monica would have sympathised, what with her feeling exactly the same. Try as she might, Monica couldn't get any words out: it all seemed too complicated.

It'd been a late night for Paddy, he'd had fun with Nicci Sharma. After the bar they'd moved on to a nightclub where they danced and drank until the early morning. He'd slept through the morning with every intention of missing out the afternoon too, but the insistent ringing of the phone succeeded in waking him up. He shuffled into the small kitchen-cum-business-powerhouse, yawning as he stretched away the bleariness. He wore yesterday's T-shirt and boxers, and a face of concern: 'Monica, are you alright?'

Monica stared at the phone with disgust, as though it was the machine itself that had insulted her in her own home. 'The Boot Camp Dan nutcases have got my number:

not only are they emailing me their abuse, they're phoning me up too now.'

As if on cue, the phone buzzed, startling them both. They shared a glance, and Paddy gave her a reassuring nod, as if to say, 'It's okay, I'm here.' Gingerly, she lifted the phone and pressed 'accept'.

'Good morning, *We Sit P*—'

'Don't you put the phone down on me you miserable old cow, we know where you live, we'll get you for what you—'

Paddy snatched the phone from her. 'Just ignore it, Monica. I'll speak with Nicci again, let her know it's getting worse. Maybe she can do something.'

Paddy wasn't an insensitive soul, in fact being one of those freaks of nature who'd been blessed with a happy-go-lucky, carefree life he was actually very empathetic to other people's plights: he saw the distress riven through his sister and it pained him. 'I'm so sorry Monica, it's so unfair, this shouldn't be happening to you. We'll get it sorted, I promise.'

Appreciating her brother's kindness, she shut her eyes and took a deep breath: *stay cool, think smart, I can get through this*. 'Thanks, Paddy. It'll all be fine,' she said with convincing confidence.

Yet again the phone rang. It shook and buzzed in Paddy's hand like an angry wasp. Monica gasped a silent 'oh no'; tears welled in her eyes. Anger coursed through him, filling his veins with red-hot lava. He jabbed the phone and raised it to his ear: 'Listen to me and listen closely Numbskull, the police have been informed, they've fitted this number with tracking software and they know your location. We'll see you in court!'

'Oh, I'm sorry. I think I must have a wrong number,' replied a timid mousey voice, 'I was after the pet people, you see I'm calling in response to their advert.'

PADDY SHUFFLED AWKWARDLY, foot to foot. He didn't like formal dress, in fact he didn't even know he possessed a tie until Monica brandished it at him, excavated from the deepest recesses of his closet: a flowery colourful thing he didn't recognise and could never imagine owning. Monica was insistent she'd bought it for him to wear at a cousin's wedding two years ago last June; right or wrong she seemed very certain and he couldn't be bothered to argue. Reluctantly he put it on.

'Why am I here?' he hissed at her. The door remained firmly sealed in front of them. Monica pressed the bell push again and like before, the chimes of Big Ben sounded far off inside the house.

'Because this is our first client enquiry,' hissed Monica straight back at him. 'You want to be a director of *We Sit Pets*, then you need to front up for the clients.'

Paddy tracked back over conversations from the past few days: *did I say that? I never said I wanted that?* But again, he couldn't be bothered to argue and let it drop.

A timid mousey voice called from deep within the house, the sound muffled by the solid door, but just about clear enough to let them know someone was coming.

'That's okay, dear, you take your time,' replied Paddy, his voice sounded naturally kind and caring. Monica immediately knew she'd made the right decision bringing him along. Allowing himself a moment to relax, safe in the knowledge the occupant was moving at a glacial speed, Paddy rocked back on his heels and let a little bounce into his knees. 'So, heard from your handsome smoothie lately?'

A warm flush prickled Monica's cheeks in response to Paddy's direct questioning. She noticed his smirk. They'd shared a lifetime of sibling friction and competition; she knew he was enjoying making her squirm. Her chosen course of action? Brazen it out. 'I assume you mean James Doyle? If so, no I haven't. I imagine he's busy in Geneva meeting his investors. I thought we'd go to his house and see his cat once we'd finished here.'

Paddy hadn't expected that. He was hoping for a light embarrassment with a touch of teasing, not more work. The lure of his bed and the prospect of sleeping off last night's frivolities appealed far more than house calls and cat food. 'Really? Surely you don't need me too? Can't I go home?'

'Certainly not!' she snapped back. 'In case you've forgotten, I've got nut-nut obsessives harassing me, who knows, they might even be stalking me.' Although not blessed with Paddy's sense of empathy, even Monica could spot the wavering between resentment at being made to work against his concern for her safety conflict across his conscience. 'Stay with me, Paddy. Please. I'm worried.'

'Alright, Monica. We'll only stay five minutes to feed the cat and then come straight home though. Hopefully Nicci will get us some help soon.'

'Okay, thanks, Paddy.'

At the moment of reaching mutual agreement, the door finally cracked open an inch. It released a fiery blast of central heating. A rheumy eye peered through. 'Oh yes, you must be the pet people.'

PADDY WASN'T COMFORTABLE. The room was far too hot. The house smelt like a launderette. The button at his collar dug into his throat; he was convinced the tie Monica had made him wear was cutting off the blood supply to his brain. Surreptitiously he cast his eyes to the floor, looking for somewhere soft to fall when he eventually passed out: either through oxygen deprivation, or total boredom.

A footstep or two in front of him, Monica was unaware of her brother's discomfort. She was, however, in her absolute element. Dressed in her sharpest business suit she wielded her tablet device like a weapon: bringing up colourful slides, impressive-looking charts and whizzy graphics. This was her opportunity to shine, this was what Martin the Ignoramus had been holding her back from all these years, this was her presentation, her pitch, her chance for glory in the boardroom.

Except it wasn't a boardroom. It was a chintzy, cluttered living room in a small overheated house that smelt of too much tumble-drying.

MRS PATTISON PRIDED HERSELF on her manners and so didn't like to interrupt the young woman, although she was beginning to worry she'd seen eighty-three Christmases and if the girl didn't get a move on she might drift off without seeing another. The gadget the girl held was bright and colourful but Mrs Pattison had forgotten to put on her readers; she had no idea what she was meant to be looking at. The girl talked too much and too quickly and used silly long words that made no sense. Every now and again she'd chirp in with a 'Yes dear,' and a 'That's nice,' when it seemed appropriate. The rest of the time she looked at the handsome young man behind. His glossy black hair reminded her of her Jim, back when they were first courting. Jim was still doing his apprenticeship back then. During the week he'd go to the depot in his overalls but on a weekend he'd come calling in his Burton's suit, his black hair slicked back; he fancied it made him look like Billy J. Kramer. She knew this young pair won't have a clue who Billy J. Kramer was, but he was quite the dish back in the day. Much like the nice young man in front of her.

' ... and that's why *We Sit Pets* is the ideal choice to take care of all your animal welfare needs.'

'Yes dear, that's nice,' replied Mrs Pattison. The girl looked expectantly at her. She wanted something: *oh, has she finished, I wasn't listening, and now she's pulling papers from her briefcase. They look official. Oh dear. Susan always says Mum don't sign anything without me there and don't buy from anyone on the doorstep, but Muffin needs his walks and I can't do it anymore, not with my ankles and Susan's too busy what with her new job and the kids.*

PADDY HADN'T FELT THIS uncomfortable in a long time. Ties, what's the point of ties? Ties were why he hated job interviews so much; that, and the actual prospect of getting a job. He'd spotted a pile of old magazines and newspapers and selected it as the point for his collapse; it looked fairly soft compared to all the dark brown wooden furniture and Lladró that filled the room. He gave his neck another roll, trying to work the button away from garrotting him when he noticed movement around his feet. Something furry, pewter coloured and roughly the size and shape of a football barrelled into his shins. He glanced down again and realised it was an obese and overindulged pug.

MONICA HELD THE CONTRACT in front of her as tightly as she held the rictus grin. She'd spotted all the buying signals from the old woman; she'd been hooked by Monica's ace presentation. Now all she needed to do was sign the paperwork and We Sit Pets would have its first official client.

MRS PATTISON CAUGHT SIGHT of Muffin snuffling around the feet of the young man: *oh, there you are, I wondered where you'd got to. You seem very keen on him, Muffin. What a lot of attention you're giving him. Must be a good sign, dogs are the best judge of character, that's what my Jim always used to say.* She watched on as the young man dropped to a squat. He took Muffin's face in his hands, looked into the dog's eyes and wiggled his nose at him.

PADDY COULDN'T STOP HIMSELF. Before he knew what he was doing he was down on his haunches taking the pug's squishy fat face in his hands, 'Hello darling, how are you today?' he cooed, wiggling his nose in front of its face. The pug snuffled noisily in delight. Without looking up he simply knew Monica's eyes burned in to him. A telling-off afterwards was likely, and he was convinced he'd be hearing words like *amateur* and *unprofessional* and *idiot* – especially *idiot* – thrown at him like knives.

MUFFIN SEEMED BESOTTED by the young man, and made wiggling figure-eights around his legs. Muffin liked the young man, and he liked Muffin: that was good enough for Mrs Pattison. She took the papers from the girl's outstretched hand, and even without her readers on she signed her name at the bottom of the page: *We Sit Pets* had its first official client.

ONCE OUTSIDE, PADDY didn't get the onslaught of insults he been expecting from his sibling. By the same token, Monica was equally surprised she didn't get the lashings of praise she was expecting from hers: didn't he appreciate a business superhero when he saw one in action? *He's lucky I was there with my commercial know-how to rescue our pitch after that display by him. It was unprofessional, made us look amateurs, the idiot!*

THEY HEADED HOME in an uncomfortable silence, neither quite knowing what the other was thinking but neither crediting their first victory solely to the very curious nose of a roly-poly old dog.

HOME AGAIN. PADDY removed his tie, popped open his collar button. The blood flow found its way back to his extremities; he welcomed the sensation of having ears again. Monica brought over two mugs of tea she'd just made, and sat down. Paddy, much to his delight, had just discovered a packet of chocolate digestives in the back of the cupboard; hidden by Monica who'd been saving them. He brought them to the table, having virtually inhaled two of them before he'd even sat down. He noticed what

Monica was intending to do: 'No, don't do it Mon, you'll only upset yourself,' but she'd already raised the phone to her ear.

She flapped a hand. 'I'm only checking voicemails, it'll be fine.'

It wasn't fine.

'Message one: "We know where you live, Monica Minton, we'll make you suffer like ..." Message deleted. Message two: "Ms Minton, this is Detective Inspector Canning. I have a number of questions that require answering, if you could ..." Message deleted.'

Paddy was reaching for his fifth chocolate digestive but Monica was on her feet, putting her jacket back on and hoiking her bag across her shoulder. 'Come on Paddy, we're going out.'

'But, Mon—'

'Now, Paddy. Get a move on.'

IT MUST HAVE MADE boring viewing. Monica Minton and her brother were watched, all dolled up to the nines like they were going to a wedding. They left their house to visit an old woman's house three doors up. It neared the hour mark of being stuck in the car going steadily brain-dead at the inane chatter of the radio host and the strain on the bladder getting distinctly uncomfortable: perhaps it was time to give up and drive away. Just then, the Mintons came out and returned to their own home, however it was merely minutes before they were out again. They got into a car and pulled away: the sister drove, the brother the passenger. With thoughts of bursting bladders set aside, and managing to stay at least three cars distant like people do on the telly, the Mintons were followed to a pay and display car park close to the town centre. Fortunately, a space was available a row over from the Mintons' parking spot enabling an ordinary, unremarkable car to slot in unnoticed and maintain the tail; on foot this time. The Mintons made the short walk to the nearby pedestrianised High Street but kept on straight past the grand department store on the corner, past the shops and past the cafés, finally stopping outside a modern red-brick office building.

To any passers-by the window-shopper was deliberating over the wide, varied selection of colourful cupcakes the bakery was famous locally for. It was however in fact a convenient vantage point to study the young couple by the office building doorway up ahead; providing a clear unimpeded view. The dark-haired young woman stooped slightly to speak into a voice-box beside the door. Anything she may have said was lost in the tide of traffic noise, but whatever it was must have worked: the door opened under her gentle push. She stepped inside, followed by her brother, then they were gone from view.

Breaking cover from the bakery and scurrying over to the door now firmly shut, the brass plate attached to the door was studied with urgent attention. That was enough;

nature was calling too loudly to be ignored anymore. Remembering a burger joint passed by earlier, a quick scuttle back up the street and a visit to its facilities put a very swollen bladder at ease. The relief sweeping through was only momentary, swiftly replaced by determination. The brass plate had read *"Irving, Pickering & Smith: Solicitors".* Something needed to be done, and done immediately.

CHAPTER **FOURTEEN**

JAMES DOYLE'S PLACE WAS AT THE TOP OF A GENTLE HILL, the toe-end of a gated cul-de-sac: one of nine built about fifteen years ago in a modern faux-historic style involving yellow bricks and lots of stone details. All had neat lawns, mature trees and shiny new SUVs: the staple of the stockbroker-belt stay-at-home mum. James Doyle's was easy to spot: it was the only one with a bare driveway. Clearly, he'd driven himself to the airport rather than getting a cab.

Monica walked around the side of the house and at the back came to a wide terrace with cast iron furniture. Following James's instructions, she found the small key-box fixed discreetly and out of sight to a low retaining wall planted with glossy-leafed shrubs. Using the combination dials, she entered the code and – hey presto – it opened; inside were two silver keys and a brass one. As promised, the brass one fitted the lock to the nearest door. It swung open and Monica stepped inside, into a compact, narrow utility room. It had one internal door, set directly opposite, and through that she was into the main home, finding herself in the kitchen. The owner's swift departure was evident: toast crumbs on the worktop, an unwashed plate and mug in the sink – but her focus was squarely on the floor tiles, the impressive island feature and the sounds beyond that: *where are you, Uncle Albert?* Monica crouched and used a tone she hoped sounded coaxing: 'Come out, come out, wherever you are.'

'I'm right here,' replied Paddy, following her into the kitchen. His right arm was clutched across his body diagonally, pinning something tight to his chest. It made him look like a rugby player, a rugby player that is if the balls these days are soft and white and fluffy.

'I assume this is who you're looking for?' He gently placed the cat on the floor in a corner laid out with feeding bowls and a basket. 'Here you go, mate,' Paddy gave a wiffle of the fluffy cat's quiff of white hair. Uncle Albert responded with an appreciative purr that sounded as though someone faraway in a different street had revved up a motorcycle.

Monica approached, squatted and reached out to stroke the cat. In the blink of a hummingbird's eye the purring stopped and a set of vicious talons swatted away her hand. Uncle Albert bared his fangs in a loud hiss, then shot away through a door left ajar. On the back of Monica's hand three parallel lines, each about an inch long, began to bead. First came droplets of blood, then came the stinging sensation. With a most unladylike swear she thrust her hand out over the kitchen sink and turned the water on full bore.

'You're a natural, Mon,' said Paddy, seizing on the opportunity to torment his sister: it was almost nostalgic, just like old times.

Monica dabbed her hand dry with a paper towel. The shock of the cold water had stemmed the blood and numbed the sting. 'Where'd he go?'

'Through that door over there,' Paddy squished a packet of pink spongey meat into an empty bowl, 'Et voilà, dinner is served. Come on, let's go.'

'No, we need to find him. If we're looking after him for a few days we don't want him scared of us.' Monica pushed open the same door Uncle Albert was last seen sprinting through. She came into a wide panelled hall with a dining room visible through an adjacent open doorway. Daylight bled from beneath a closed door at the end of the hall, and on her left, a staircase strung with balusters in a turned pale wood. She passed down the hall making barely a sound, her footsteps silenced by the plush carpet. The house was deathly quiet, not even a ticking clock or the muted gurgle of a central heating pipe, much less the noise of a cat that wanted to be left alone.

Monica surveyed the dining room, dropping to her hands and knees to check under the table and chairs: no trace of Uncle Albert. Paddy placed a shaky hand on the pale wood newel post, seeking to balance himself on the third step of the stairs. It wasn't ideal, but snooping around someone's empty home didn't sit comfortably with him; any further up the stairs seemed like intruding. On tiptoes, stretching as far as he could go, he managed to peer over the edge of the stair-opening to the floor above. He saw a broad square landing. Several panelled doors led off, all firmly closed: 'I don't think he's upstairs, Monica.'

Monica reached for the handle of the closed door at the end of the hall, but Paddy voiced his objection. 'You shouldn't be doing that, Mon.'

'We've looked everywhere else.'

'But the door's shut, Mon. Are you suggesting the cat opened the door, went in and closed it behind him? What do you suppose he's doing, looking for somewhere quiet to enjoy a good book? No, Mon, if that door's closed it means you're not meant to be in there.'

Too late. Despite hearing Paddy's concerns, she wasn't listening. The door opened; inside was a home study-cum-office. It was small but neat and professional. A stylish desk in a pale wood, a brand-new top-of-the-range Apple computer sat astride it with the largest, thinnest screen on the market. A huge padded leather swivel chair rested behind the desk. A glass-doored bookcase took up half a wall but didn't contain many books; instead shelves of matching lever arch folders neatly labelled and numbered.

'Nice,' thought Monica to herself, 'I wouldn't mind something like this at home for me. A place to run my empire from.'

Paddy couldn't shake off his discomfort. 'Monica, get out of there,' he whispered despite no-one else being in the house to hear them. A yowl caused them both to spin around. From out of nowhere Uncle Albert strutted across the room with the kind of confident swagger that suggested he owned the place, which – as any cat-person knows – he did. He stopped and sat in the centre of the carpet where he threw a hind leg, stiff and straight, over his shoulder and bowed his head. He resembled a tiny cellist and both Mintons witnessed his ablutions in absolute silence. When satisfied with his preening, a fluffy white sashay brought him across to Paddy. He rubbed himself against Paddy's shins with another Harley-Davidson purr. Uncle Albert rolled onto his back exposing a soft white belly, and accepting the invitation Paddy dropped on his haunches and began to tickle.

A shade of envy fell across Monica: *I'm not going to stand here like a gooseberry while he gets loved-up with the stupid cat.* Her eyes swept the room again; this time her attention landed on a folder neatly positioned squarely on the desk: *Boot Camp Dan*, the spine label stated. Paddy was engrossed with the cat and unlikely to voice any objection, even if he'd noticed her flip it open and start reading. The first few pages were spreadsheet printouts, this was her forte, she devoured the contents and with a wistful twinge realised how much she missed the corporate world. The figures represented the full extent of James's investment in Boot Camp Dan. With her expertise, she easily identified his actual costs spent so far. It was a value so substantial her eyebrows were at risk of altitude sickness.

In the car afterwards Monica tried explaining the sheer size and significance of it to Paddy. She didn't let herself get frustrated by the ignorance he took pride in. Rather, she saw it as good training opportunity. Convinced it was an invaluable business skill, she accepted the challenge she'd set herself: simplify a myriad of complex interlocking transactions and strategies into a language so plain and basic the layman back on the street could understand – and let's face it, there's no man on any street more laid-back than Paddy Minton. He got it on the first attempt, much to her delight but also, she found, to her annoyance. Sibling rivalry and childish competitive streaks that spanned a lifetime flared up again. She found herself conflicted: on the one hand she brimmed with smugness for succeeding so well in her challenge, but on the other there simmered a resentment that he'd picked up at his first attempt what it had taken her years of hard work plus a university degree to master.

'So, what's Smoothie do now?' asked Paddy. 'Write it all off as bad luck and take the hit?'

'No,' replied Monica, ignoring the deliberate jibe. 'He was smart enough to take out insurance.' She saw the askance grimace pulled by Paddy, and she explained further, 'A kind of business interruption insurance. I expect it'll be a hard fight, and take a bit of argument, but he should be able to claim most of his money back.'

'So what's Geneva all about then? Why the sudden rush to get the first flight out there?'

Monica thought how to respond for a moment before realising she didn't actually know, so gave it her best guess: 'Reputation, I assume. He said they are big, big money people. I imagine he thinks the most respectful thing to do is apologise to them in person and reassure them it won't happen again. If he's no longer considered a safe pair of hands, they'll de-risk and take their money to someone else.' She was quite pleased with her best guess, but she could have said anything; Paddy was on autopilot, he'd given up listening ages ago and was looking forward to getting home for his nap.

THE TRAFFIC WAS LIGHT and moved freely. Within twenty minutes they'd reached the final junction and turned in, towards home. Monica's house was halfway along a charming terrace of flat-fronted Victorian houses on a dead-end lane that remained popular and in demand with house-proud young professionals. Perhaps house-proud may have been an understatement; for a long while the prissy chair of the residents' committee had been canvassing support from her members, as she wanted to draft a strongly worded letter to Miss Minton at number seven: this is a historically important location and as custodians of it, we need to maintain its aesthetic, or words to that effect. The Prissy Chair didn't like living next door to Monica, believing she lowered the tone of the street. She didn't care that Monica left the house at six every morning and returned at eight every night; other people managed to paint their woodwork, clean their windows and keep their bins out of sight, why couldn't she? By pure luck and coincidence for Monica, a nurse she'd never met saved her from the much threatened strongly worded letter.

Romance had come knocking for a lad named Mike in the form of a feisty little nurse called Preeti, and Preeti didn't want Mike's slacker of a flatmate cluttering up their love-nest. Responding to her ultimatum, Mike was forced to tell his old friend Paddy (for it was he) that it was time for him to go. Needing somewhere to stay, Monica, coerced and cajoled by her mother, agreed to let Paddy stay at hers; *just a couple of weeks though, Paddy, okay?* That was over two years ago. But the arrangement worked, both of them operating on different time zones, so they barely saw each other. They had the regular arguments about rent, or rather lack of it, but as Paddy would always point out, 'You managed to pay the mortgage and the bills perfectly well on your own without me, so what difference does it make to you now?' Monica had a valid response, but she knew she was wasting her breath when even their own mother, acting as an "independent" adjudicator, stated: *well, he does make a very good point, darling.*

Paddy however was not totally insensitive. He tried in his own way to be a good tenant and house guest: what he lacked in cash, he tried to make up for in action. Monica may not have noticed, but the neighbours did: her grimy stonework was cleaned and whitewashed, her fading front door painted a vibrant buttercup yellow, the dead and droopy bizzy-lizzies replaced with a colourful hanging basket. When Monica left the house to put her nose against the grindstone of commerce every day, Paddy transformed it. Within a month he'd brought it up to the standard of the others in the lane, within three months he'd exceeded it. Monica's house shone like a little jewel halfway along the attractive, quaint terrace. The neighbours approved, even the Prissy Chair next door. In fact, the Prissy Chair had become a firm convert, with any thoughts of a strongly worded letter forgotten – although that may have had more to do with the time last summer when standing by her window she saw a shirtless Paddy tending Monica's garden; he looked up, noticed her and gave her a wave and the famous Paddy smile. That was it, she was firmly Team Minton; *what charming neighbours I have, I'm so lucky.*

NICCI SHARMA WAS DETERMINED to work through the dull throb poking her in the head. It'd been a fun night with Paddy, but now she was suffering for it. It'd been a struggle to stay awake in Canning's meeting this morning, and now back at her desk the words on her screen didn't stop swimming around no matter how hard she concentrated. She began to read the same sentence for the fourth time when her phone rang.

"Paddy M" declared the caller ID; *just the distraction I need. S*he picked up the phone, answered it and leaned back in her chair, looking forward to a pleasant diversion away from her reports and statements.

'Nicci ... our house, it's been ransacked. They've trashed it!'

CHAPTER **FIFTEEN**

AS FAR AS HANGOVER CURES GO, I GUESS IT WORKS, thought Nicci Sharma; the fog in her thoughts were instantly expelled the moment Paddy spoke, the adrenaline rush replacing the headache with her sense of duty: 'Don't touch anything, Paddy. I'll be straight over.'

True to her word she was in the car by the time she'd finished the call, and in the ring-road traffic just minutes later. The route was quick and clear, no need for flashing lights; it took less than ten minutes, but the drive gave her chance to reflect on last night. Their date, as it was, was brief but enjoyable. Both seemed easy in each other's company; relaxed, with just that little fizzle of electric tension. It felt good.

She drove fast, pushing the small unmarked hatchback hard. Before long she came to a halt, halfway along a charming terrace: *nice place, wish I could afford to live here,* she noted to herself. Nicci's detective instincts immediately sensed something awry. The lane was clearly full of house-proud young professionals. No doubt their interiors would be just as fashionably decorated with every modern appliance, and then some. If it was a run-of-the-mill opportunist burglar, why pick Monica's halfway along the street when others offered easier access or were less overlooked?

Monica and Paddy were waiting on the pavement outside, both wearing suits: *he looks pretty fine suited and booted,* she mused, then admonished herself, *get your mind on work, Nic.*

They greeted her wordlessly. Nicci responded with a nod designed to convey calm professionalism. Standing slightly apart from the Minton siblings, Nicci studied the small terraced house. Flanked both sides by adjoining identical houses, the narrow frontage was only wide enough for the entrance door, and the window to the front room. A quick up-and down glance: no damage to the door. Eyes flicked right for a similar scan: original Victorian sash window, flimsy and insecure, but again no sign of damage or forced entry. The tight confines of the entrance hallway made it dark and heavy with shadow. Even through a squint it took a moment or two for Nicci's eyes to adjust to the low light. Then she saw it.

The hallway was in fact a corridor, running a straight line from the front of the house to the back. At the very end, the proverbial light at the end of the tunnel: the kitchen window, smashed. Shards of glass scattered across the countertop and floor. It twinkled in the darkness; far away stars emerging from the dusk. Something dark and angular looked out of place on the countertop: a half-brick. There couldn't be any doubt: it'd come through the window.

Nicci, satisfied a break-in had taken place, made a phone call.

'I've called for a forensic team, they're sending someone out. They'll be here very soon, Monica. But can you tell me, are you hurt?' Monica shook her head in response to Nicci's question, and Paddy mouthed a silent 'Thank you.'

Paddy sat Monica in the passenger seat of her own car and Nicci spoke to him across the roof of it, 'Paddy, are they still in the house?'

'I don't know. We opened the door, saw the window smashed and called you straight away. We haven't been in yet. We didn't know what to do so stayed by the door 'til you turned up.'

Nicci took this as her cue and returned back to the house. Slowly, methodically, she surveyed the rooms. The adrenalin and danger made her veins run hot, every footstep taking aeons, every creak of the old building heightening her senses further. In real time Paddy and Monica were only waiting a matter of minutes at the car before she was back with them.

'It's clear. Nobody there,' she informed them, 'and doesn't look like they took anything.'

Paddy wore a quizzical look. To the best of his knowledge, she'd never been in Monica's house before. 'How can you know that?'

'Obviously you'll need to check for yourself but first impressions, nothing looks out of place,' replied Nicci. 'All drawers and cupboard doors neatly shut, no sign of rummaging. The TV is there, and a games console. Upstairs in the bedroom I saw a jewellery box and a nice watch on the dressing table, a pile of coins beside the bed. Any thief would have taken all of that.'

'So, it wasn't a break-in? Just a random vandal smashing windows?'

'I didn't say that, Paddy. Whoever it was, they put through kitchen window then reached through to unlock the door. They came in. That back room, the kitchen diner? Does it have another use?'

'Monica's office.'

'Thought so. They've smashed up a laptop computer, and snapped a tablet device in two. And there's tons of paper tossed all over the floor. They've certainly made a mess.'

'What's it mean, do you think?'

Nicci took his elbow and led him away from the car. Satisfied they were out of Monica's earshot, she continued, 'In my opinion, this wasn't an opportunist thief. This was targeted. Any idea who?'

Paddy's eyes widened, his astonishment evident. 'Boot Camp Dan! The messages said they knew where we lived. Do you think they've tried to destroy *We Sit Pets* by smashing up all the business equipment?'

This time Nicci's eyes widened. 'Paddy, are you sure? They said that, they actually said they know where you live?'

Paddy stepped back, opened the car door and leaned in to Monica. She handed him her phone, which he brought back to Nicci. He replayed the voicemail messages for Nicci's benefit. 'That's enough for us to launch a full investigation for harassment. Leave it with me, I'll get our tech team to trace the incoming messages.'

Paddy looked to Monica; she jotted down her number and passwords on the back of Nicci Sharma's card. Nicci slipped it into her jacket pocket, 'I'll get back to you as soon as I can, okay?'

A patrol car arrived and two uniforms stepped out. Paddy recognised them, the same two that he'd met before; the small rotund female and the slim male with the eyes that never blinked.

'I'll take care of these guys,' offered Nicci. 'Is there somewhere safe where Monica can go tonight?'

'My Mum's,' replied Paddy. 'We'll spend the night there.'

'Great. I'll call you in the morning and we can organise her statement for the crime report, okay.'

Paddy reached for Nicci's hand. He gave a small squeeze. 'Thanks, for everything,' he said, then planted a soft kiss on her cheek.

Nicci looked away from the open-mouthed surprise of her sparrow-shaped female colleague and barked some unnecessarily over-harsh instructions to the male officer to deflect any further gawping. The officers got about their business. With their backs turned and attention elsewhere

Nicci exchanged goodbye waves with Paddy as he got into the driver's seat of Monica's car and pulled away from the kerb. She watched until the car turned at the end of the lane, then it was back to work.

'... SO IF YOU COULD keep looking after him I'd be very grateful, thanks. And look after yourself, it sounds awful.' Then, nothing. Dead air. The call had been cut.

James Doyle, calling from Geneva, wanted to hear how his cat was coping without him. Instead, he'd had a twenty-minute emotional download from a distraught Monica. Uncle Albert, his fluffy white gentleman of senior years, was fine. When you're an over-indulged blob of white fluff that resembles a cushion on a sofa more than a lion on a plain, life is generally pretty fine most of the time. As long as you're fed three times a day and you've a sunny spot out of the draught to curl up in, things are going grand. For Monica however, things most definitely weren't going grand. After making what he'd judged a polite quantity of sympathetic noises he pounced on the next pause he spotted and gabbled his quick farewell.

'Was that the Handsome Smoothie?' asked Paddy, knowing the answer already. He'd heard her use his name several times, but he thought maybe a conversation could free Monica from the cloud she seemed trapped under.

'Mmmm,' her reply was half-hearted, her mind still elsewhere. 'He needs to spend another day in Geneva, he says he can't get a meeting with his contact until the morning and he's asked if we can look after Uncle Albert for another day.'

'Great news, *We Sit Pets* gets its contract renewed.' Paddy used more bravado than the response merited. It got a quizzical look from Monica. 'I'm just trying to find a positive, Monica, that's all.'

'I know, Paddy, I know.' Monica looked around her home. 'Will you stay for a bit please? Help me tidy up?'

After spending the night at their mother's, in the bed she used to sleep in as a teenager, she was ready to come home. Paddy brought her back to her own house, and opening up for her he saw the chaos with his own eyes. Nicci hadn't exaggerated: they'd gone berserk in the back room. As soon as he'd seen the mess, he had written off his morning's plans, knowing she would need help getting it cleared, he just hadn't volunteered himself yet. So, when asked, he nodded straight away.

Monica smiled and placed a light hand on his shoulder. 'Thanks, Paddy. I knew you would. Let me put the kettle on, and then we can get started.'

The kettle hubbled and bubbled. Monica flicked on a radio; the soothing regional accent of the host murmured before launching into a bouncy pop hit from the 80's. Neither of them was particularly interested but it made for a bit of background, and added a thin veneer of normalcy to the proceedings. Paddy cleared up all the broken and damaged stuff; Monica gathered the spilled papers, trying to restructure them into some kind of order.

A little over an hour, and the room was tidy once more. Paddy eyed a nearby armchair with desire. He'd just hauled a heavy sack of detritus out into the compact courtyard garden at the back: *that'll do for now, I'll take it down the tip later, but first I think another cup of tea's in order.* The doorbell rang*: oh bugger!*

'Monica? ... Monica?' called Paddy, who'd sat down and couldn't be bothered getting up again. 'Monica?'

Monica's voice travelled from upstairs, 'I'm on the phone with the insurance.'

Paddy winced through the stiffness that had formed in his lower back and hauled himself out of his armchair. He opened the door to find a small, stocky man in camouflage trousers who he greeted with an odd sensation: part confusion, part familiarity. The man clutched a substantial toolbox in one hand; the other rubbed back and forth across his shaved head: 'Morning! Glazier,' he said by way of introduction.

'Ah yes, of course, I forgot you were coming. This way, mate,' Paddy led him through to the kitchen, and the offending smashed window. 'I'd just put the kettle on. Want one?'

MONICA HAD JUST ABOUT lost the will to live. For more than half an hour she'd been navigating the automated menus of her insurer's claim line. Thirty-six minutes, in fact, she noted catching a glance at the clock beside the bed. All she wanted was a real-life human being to speak to; was that too much to ask? Don't they make them anymore? 'No no no,' she yelled at the robot voice asking if she was calling to renew her motoring policy. It connected her anyway. Giving up, she went with the flow, letting the computers decide where to go next. To her utter amazement a real-life human being began speaking to her. The human being introduced himself as Gavin. Monica introduced herself as Monica and explained about her broken window and her smashed computer equipment.

'And where was the vehicle parked?' asked Gavin.

'What vehicle?'

'The vehicle with the broken window. Where was the vehicle parked: driveway, garage, or public highway?' asked Gavin, valiantly sticking to his script.

'It's a two-bedroom terraced house.'

'So that'd be public highway then, would it?'

'No. My house has the broken window.'

'Are you claiming against someone else's insurance? Their driving caused damage to your property? I must advise you will have needed to have exchanged insurance details and taken photographs at the scene of the accident if you wish to prove liability.'

'No. My house was burgled—'

'This is motor insurance, madam. You need home cover. That's a different department, let me put you through.'

'No, wait, no—'

Too late. The jaunty instrumental orchestra played again; this time *'Don't Cry for Me Argentina'* but just as it was getting to the good bit the robot voice interrupted: 'If you would like to take part in our short survey—' The phone hit the wall with such speed and force it'd make a spin bowler green with envy.

'I must be able to do it online, surely,' muttered Monica to herself, wondering whether anyone would notice if she added her now shattered phone to her insurance claim.

'WHAT DO YOU RECKON, Monica, looks as good as new doesn't it?'

Monica had descended the stairs enraged. The insurance robots had beaten her and she wanted to lash out. When she found Paddy and his new friend sipping tea and eating the last of her chocolate digestives, she knew she'd found her target. Her fury had locked on and was ready for launch in three ... two ... what? Paddy's gleeful grin distracted her; her attention followed the jut of his chin. For reasons unexplained, the anger and resentment inside dissipated at the sight facing her: a shining, crystal clear window pane where once an angry jagged hole terrified her.

'Quite pleased with it, myself,' said the man in the armchair next to Paddy, 'I like doing these old houses, doing it the traditional old-fashioned way.'

'Thanks—' Monica felt like she should know his name, there was something familiar about him, but no name was forthcoming. 'How much do I owe you?'

TEN MINUTES AND a swipe of the credit card later, the glazier was gone; off to his next booking. Monica returned to the kitchen, and flicked the kettle switch. It was becoming one of those mornings when the kettle never cools down. She didn't bother asking Paddy, knowing full well what his response would be. She carried the two mugs to the table, pushing one across to Paddy, who took it with eager rapture.

'Eugh ... builder's ... must be yours,' Monica's nose wrinkled at the taste. She swapped it with the one she'd given Paddy and took a sip. The flowery taste of Earl Grey bloomed in her mouth, eliciting a sigh of satisfaction from her. She gazed through her new window, at the chimney pots of the houses behind. 'He did do a very neat job, that guy. Where'd you find him, Paddy? Friend of yours?'

Paddy gave a gentle head shake, 'No, I simply did a search for local glaziers, he was the first one to the answer the phone.'

'I just assumed he was a mate of yours. He reminded me of someone, but I couldn't put my finger on it.'

'I thought that too. When I saw him on the doorstep, at first I thought it was Pete.' Paddy knew from Monica's expression she was struggling. 'Pete. Birdwatching Pete. From the riverside park, Pete the sniper.'

'Yes, of course, that's who.' Monica's relief at solving that little mystery sounded evident in her response. 'It's the camouflage, isn't it? He never wears anything else.'

Paddy took a cautious sip from his tea to test its temperature. It was his fifth cup of the morning and his teeth had started to feel furry, but it didn't put him off. He took a thirsty gulp, then: 'Yes he does. Remember when he turned up looking dapper in his new shirt and trousers.'

Monica cast her mind back. Paddy was right; Pete had turned up in his camper van, looking freshly shaved and showered and dressed smartly in clean clothes: wait, what day was it?

'Paddy? Do you remember when we saw him like that? Was it the day of Boot Camp Dan's murder?'

'Yeah, that's right, what about it?'

Sometimes Monica despaired of her brother. This was such a time. She'd hoped he'd fill in the logic himself, but she could see she'd need to walk him through it step by step.

'Think about it Paddy,' she began. 'Take it from the beginning: running into him, absolutely livid at Boot Camp Dan's shenanigans, furious about the effect on the birdlife. Then at the Munsters', shouting his mouth off about Boot Camp Dan and admitting to daydreams about assassinating him. We were all at the Munsters' listening to him, he storms off in a rage, we don't see him again until after Boot Camp Dan's bludgeoned to death, and when we do see him he's all freshly laundered.'

Paddy sat transfixed, his mouth open and slack. Monica could tell a lot of processing was happening behind his eyes: 'You think Pete killed Boot Camp Dan?'

'Come on, Paddy. It all fits. He's a trained killer. He's been on the receiving end of Boot Camp Dan's bullying ways for ages, hasn't he. Remember, he said Boot Camp Dan got the birdwatching club moved on from their location and then the launch event, he called it eco-terrorism, didn't he? He was certainly angry enough, he's definitely capable enough, and the timing seems to fit.'

Paddy nodded in a loose kind of way, as if to say *the theory holds water but I'm still not one hundred per cent on board.*

'Can I borrow your phone please,' Monica extended her open palm, ready to receive.

'No way, you're not using my phone,' he protested, 'use your own.'

'No, and I don't want your proper phone, I want your secret burner phone please.' Monica thrust her extended palm at him as a gesture of impatience.

'What secret phone?'

'Oh come off it Paddy, you pick up more girls than the England Lionesses' tour bus. Of course you've got a secret phone to screen the numbers. Give it to me and stop mucking about.'

'I don't know what—' he began, but Monica thrust her extended palm at him again and it looked angry. 'Alright then,' he said in a deflated tone and pulled a basic-looking cell phone from the back pocket of his jeans.

Monica hid her amazement that her hunch had paid off, took the phone and headed back upstairs. She had someone she needed to speak to. Urgently.

CHAPTER **SIXTEEN**

'YOU SHOULD'VE BEEN HERE HALF AN HOUR AGO,' said Hazel with a gleeful tone, 'You've missed all the fun.'

Hazel sat on a park bench, squeezed between Tim and Kenton, enjoying the spring sunshine. Their dogs lay in heaps, relaxing after an hour's exercise along the river's edge. Monica and Paddy, dragged by hounds eager for their delayed perambulations, approached.

'It was all very exciting. It was like being in *Hill Street Blues*,' added Hazel, not noticing the perplexed reactions from everyone present under the age of fifty. She hadn't finished her newsflash: 'There were men with guns, a helicopter, it was all going off.' Beside her Tim and Kenton nodded their silent confirmation; this actually happened. Paddy's eyes widened, and his lips softened; keen to know more.

'They – the armed police – they came for Pete the birdwatcher,' said Kenton.

'They stormed the Visitors' Centre like they were the SAS,' added Tim.

'Pete?' Paddy's tone was incredulous until he caught Monica in his peripheral vision; she looked down at her feet and all of a sudden it made sense to Paddy. 'Oh.'

'The fella in the raincoat, Canning?' continued Tim, oblivious to Paddy's rapid discomfort. 'He followed in behind, and led poor old Pete off to the waiting van.'

'And didn't he look smug about it?' replied Hazel. Kenton mumbled agreement; his head slowly bobbed up and down, before he added, 'Claims he killed Boot Camp Dan.'

'I guess it makes sense, doesn't it?' Paddy hoped he could pass for surprised if he asked enough questions. 'He is a trained killer, after all.'

Hazel choked back a laugh. All eyes fixed on her. With composure restored she dabbed the corner of her lips with a tissue: 'You don't really believe he used to be a special forces sniper, do you?' She looked around the group for a response, not a sound was forthcoming but one wasn't needed, their faces gave them away. 'No. What all of you? Really? He was no more a sniper than I was in the Folies Bergère.'

Paddy was flummoxed. Partly because: *folly badgers?* But more by what he knew to be true: 'He told me he was in the first Gulf War.'

'He was,' replied Hazel, 'He was in the Gulf, that's true … as a mechanic.'

Monica, by a reflex reaction, repeated what she'd just heard: 'A mechanic?'

'That's right,' Hazel replied, reaching into her backpack. A Jack Russell raised a curious eyebrow but settled back down again when he saw it was only her notebook coming out and not a meaty treat. Hazel flicked through the first third of the pages, finally finding what she sought. 'Here we go: Pete.'

All around her the same single thought echoed in every head: I wonder what she's got about me in that book?

Hazel, oblivious to the paranoia she'd created amongst her colleagues, held the book open at arm's length, peered down her nose and started to read aloud: 'Lance Corporal Peter Colin Brooks. Royal Electrical and Mechanical Engineers, Vehicle Mechanic. Enlisted in 1987 for an eight-year service; including Operation Granby, also known as the first Gulf War of 1991. He was commended for his work in desert-proofing Challenger tanks. So, no, he didn't go on any top secret kill missions. He was an army mechanic.'

'Busy scraping sand out of holes where sand shouldn't go,' added Tim. He noted the silent reaction from his audience. 'Obviously that one needs a bit more work. I was talking about tanks, but thought if—'

Monica ignored Tim's lame attempt at a joke: *I don't know how he can claim to be a comedian, he hasn't got a funny bone in his body,* she thought to herself.

Tim floundered a little longer, trying to make it work as joke before finally giving it up as a bad idea. Silence descended on the group, everybody unsure what to say next, until Paddy sprung to his feet and summoned his dogs. 'Come on guys, let's go for a splash by the water.' The dogs bounced around him, brimming with excitement and anticipation. 'Come on, Monica, you too,' he said, summoning her from her seat.

'DO YOU THINK WE'VE made a terrible mistake?'

Monica twisted to view her brother full in the face but also to see behind them. Judging by the distance they'd covered it seemed safe to talk without anyone overhearing. She opened her mouth to answer him, but hadn't noticed the Labrador in her care cross lanes. Before a word was spoken, she tripped over it.

Paddy's arm flew in her direction, clamping on to hers, stopping her fall. He held tight as she steadied herself, then asked again, 'Have we made a mistake?'

Monica had herself been considering the same question, ever since they left their friends behind. She'd reached her conclusion. 'No. I don't think we have. Okay, so he's not a sniper, we got that wrong. But by pretending to everyone he was, then doesn't that prove he's a fantasist? Prone to delusions? Surely that makes him even more dangerous?'

'Maybe.' Paddy didn't sound convinced. 'I know, how about I ask Nicci?'

'I don't know, Paddy. She's already said she's not happy about us sticking our beaks in, hasn't she?'

'True. True.' Paddy chewed the inside of his cheek and let the seed of a thought roll around his head, snowballing larger and larger until fully formed: 'I've got it. Listen to this. She told me to call her because she wants—'

'Yeah, I know what she wants. She's wanted it since school, Paddy.'

'No, that's not what I meant,' Paddy replied, but he knew she was right, and rather liked the idea if truth be told. 'No, what I was I going to say was she wants your statement about the break-in at your house. So, we could arrange to meet her, you give your statement and then we chat all nice and friendly, how's things, going on holiday this year, blah blah blah, how's the Boot Camp Dan murder enquiry going?'

'That's it? That's your master plan?' if Monica didn't sound impressed, it was because Monica was not impressed. Not in the slightest. 'Oh, we're having two weeks in Palma Nova this August, by the way, arrested anyone interesting lately?' she said in cruel mimicry.

'I was thinking of being more subtle and casual about it, as you well know,' countered Paddy, keen to defend himself. 'I can be quite persuasive when I want to be.'

Monica had to admit he made a good point: Paddy's superhero power was the natural ability to charm the pants from the trees. She relented, and for lack of any better idea told him to set it up.

'She'll be here in an hour,' he advised Monica after speaking with her.

THE BIGGEST PROBLEM of arranging to meet anyone in a public park is the uncertainty of the weather. Within minutes of arranging their meeting a deafening thunderclap directly overhead sent everyone scurrying for cover. Seconds later rain fell, fast and heavy. Monica and Paddy made a run for it. The dogs were elated: tally-ho! Running ahead, the pack reverted to their hunting instinct, hardwired into them through centuries of breeding and training. These beasts were designed to be at the front of the charge leading out the horses, not a sedentary plod around a municipal playing field once a day. Seeing their chance to run, they ran. Monica and Paddy were hauled across the open field, barely staying on their feet, the leashes, as straight as steel rails, clutched in stiff outstretched arms.

'Full up, no room at all,' Paddy informed Monica. She'd arrived at the Visitors' Centre a few seconds behind Paddy; Paddy had got there several minutes behind everyone else in the area. Windswept, bedraggled and out of breath, Monica peered through the steamed-up window; it was packed to bursting. She scraped her dripping wet hair away from her face: 'What are we going to do now?'

WITH NOWHERE ELSE TO GO, they sat in Monica's car: her, Paddy and six damp and muddy dogs. The dogs panted; it fogged the windscreen. Their collective breath smelt fishy, and their coats stank of wet dog, which given the circumstances was understandable but still nonetheless unwelcome; much like whichever pooch it was with digestive problems that was puffing out eye-wateringly bad emissions.

'Open the windows, Monica.'

After several minutes cajoling, Monica relented. The windows whirred down an inch and a half and several gallons of icy cold water blew in, catching Paddy on the side of the head. A bead traced a freezing trickling path behind his ear before darting down inside his open collar. He gave a squeal, 'Close the windows, close the windows.' They whirred closed. The windscreen fogged over again, and the car filled with the stench of fishy wet dog breath and overpowering canine fart gas.

THE CAR LURCHED BACKWARDS under the sudden weight. It threw her back against the head rest. Nicci Sharma spun around in urgent surprise to discover the sopping and dishevelled Minton siblings filling her back seat. They slammed the doors and shuffled to get comfortable. A faint fishy odour wafted through the car.

'Café's full,' Paddy offered by way of explanation before Nicci could even say a word.

'It's the weather,' Monica added, as if Nicci hadn't noticed the monsoon battering a heavy metal drum solo on the roof, 'and we can't use my car to talk in because—'

'It stinks!'

'Because it's full of dogs.' Monica's tone slapped down her brother for his interruption.

Nicci stared at the two of them, and the puddles they were forming on the upholstery. 'You could've called me, Paddy. Arranged to meet somewhere else. At your house, perhaps?'

She watched the realisation show on Paddy's face, it formed with the speed of continental drift.

'Anyway, I can't take anyone's statement like this,' she informed them, 'I'm only here because your call gave me an excuse to get out of the office. I'm having one of those days; if I stayed, I'd have said something I'd regret.'

The wipers rose and fell, sweeping across then flicking away the build-up of water. A clear view across the park emerged, then one fat coin-sized dot blotted the screen, immediately followed by others, within seconds the park view was submerged only for the wipers to rise and fall, and the cycle began again.

'It's that idiot Canning,' said Nicci. 'He'd been given a right rollicking. He had to get a result or he was for it. We were all hoping it was our chance to be rid of him once and for all. But now this morning, he's got so much swagger you'd think he was king of the world. He's acting as if he's *Robocop* now he's had the chance to lead a firearms operation.'

'Is that right?' Monica wrung rainwater from her hair; it splattered against the footwell of the car.

Nicci shot her a glare, but it wasn't noticed. She resorted to a loud sigh instead, then continued her rant. 'He got an anonymous tip-off. A reliable source—' Nicci's reply was cut off by Paddy's snort. She looked at him for an explanation. He gave a small wobble of the hand then rubbed his nose, as if to excuse a cough or a sneeze. She held the look on him, refusing to break away; it made him uncomfortable and compelled him to break the silence.

'Anyway, you were saying, he got an anonymous tip about Pete.'

'I never mentioned anyone's name.' Nicci noticed the shifty glance exchanged between the Mintons. 'Do you two know something I don't?'

Monica inhaled and then exhaled slowly, composing her words before speaking: 'It wasn't anonymous. I made the call to Canning. I told him about Pete,' and so began her confession.

Nicci listened to, and considered, Monica's assumptions and suspicions. 'All sounds plausible, I suppose, I can see why Canning went for it.'

'I don't get it. Why say it was anonymous, when it wasn't?' Paddy directed his question to nobody specifically.

Nicci however had an answer ready for him. 'Because he's a glory seeker. A goal hanger. He's been under enormous pressure to solve this case. If he can claim he got a result from assessing the probability of a name dropped by an anonymous lead, that he put in the detective work to build a case for the prosecution, then it looks much better for him than just being given everything all neatly tied up in a bow from an enthusiastic amateur.'

'Makes sense, I suppose,' Paddy replied, but his attention had been stolen by what was happening in Monica's car beside them. Her small hatchback rocked side to side. At first he thought a fight had broken out, but on closer observation it appeared that Boris the golden Lab and Curly Sue were busy making Labradoodles.

Curiosity made Nicci seek out what had so fixated Paddy. She smiled at the sight of Roxy the Staffie chomping down on the passenger head rest. She tore a big chunk from it, and the sight was oddly pleasing given the way she felt towards Monica right now:

'It seems like your call to Canning saved his job,' she said with an unmistakeable tinge of regret. 'In the eyes of the senior management, he's gone from hero to zero. The man who took Boot Camp Dan's killer off the streets.'

'I wouldn't be so sure of that,' replied Monica.

'No? And why's that then?' Nicci challenged.

Monica leaned between the two front seats, and pointed dead ahead. 'Because there's Pete, over there.'

CHAPTER SEVENTEEN

'LOOK ON THE BRIGHT SIDE, MONICA, at least we're out of the rain now.'

Monica failed to see the bright side, sat as she was squashed between Paddy to her left and a drunk brought in for indecent exposure to her right. Finding herself stuck in the middle of a busy custody suite awaiting charges, Monica couldn't see any bright side. However, she could very clearly see the lecherous leers from the inebriated flasher beside her. He rummaged around in his trouser pockets and she knew he wasn't counting his change. He gave her a wink.

'Swap seats with me, Paddy. Now!'

Shuffling across to the seat vacated by her brother she found herself next to a very glassy-eyed young man. The young man gave off a distinct odour: very funky and exotic, probably on account of the copious amounts of skinny hand-rolled cigarettes he'd already smoked that day. At least he didn't bother her, in fact he was so chilled he was virtually catatonic. He stared vacantly up to the ceiling and beyond. Monica decided to join him. She raised her gaze heavenward but was brought back down to Earth by the bark of the custody sergeant.

'Monica Minton. Your solicitor has arrived. Ready for your interview?'

HOW HAD IT COME TO THIS? Monica wondered to herself, looking at the plain drab walls. She'd been ushered into the small cuboid room by the same bird-like female officer who'd come to her house the other day. She couldn't remember her name, and the officer didn't speak. Instead, she gave a wordless extension of the arm to indicate where Monica should sit. Monica duly obliged and sat on a hard, upright seat facing the door. In front of it was a small table, fixed to the wall. The female police officer took a standing position in the corner of the room, directly behind Monica. The space was cramped and constrained; from her corner position the police officer could place her hand on Monica's shoulder without even stretching. Thoughts of the officer stretching her arm, spun into fantasies about birds spreading their wings: maybe she could join the Flying Squad? Monica supressed the smile; *it's funny how your mind reacts when nervous,* she pondered.

'Won't be long now, just a couple of minutes,' the officer trilled. Monica was unsure whether she meant she'd only be held a short time longer, or whether that was before anything happened, but she didn't ask. For want of anything else to do, Monica studied the man to her left.

Unpacking a notepad from a briefcase so old the leather was as soft and supple as felt, the man, her lawyer, placed it on the table then fiddled with a fountain pen, unscrewing and screwing the cap. Constrained by the poky space, she had no choice but give the man close inspection:

nearing retirement age, his dry white hair thinned at the back but sharp thick barbs sprouted in his ears. His heavy-framed glasses, out of fashion by many, many years, were smudged. Monica thought back to meeting him a day or so ago: *he seemed so confident behind his desk, now he looks more nervous than me.*

She closed her eyes, and tried to remember her mindful techniques: *look for the happy place, look for the happy place.* Unfortunately visions of the happy place weren't forthcoming, the only thing in the darkness behind her eyelids was the events of the morning repeating on a constant replay.

THEY'D BEEN SITTING in Nicci's car. The rain on the roof sounded like a troop of tap dancers falling down a metal staircase: '… there's Pete over there,' said Monica.

The wide eaves of the Visitors' Centre gave just about enough overhang to provide shelter from the worst of the rain, as long as you stood close to the wall and didn't move. And there, at the end of the invisible line extending from Monica's fingertip, lurked Pete: next to a fire exit door, dressed in his customary camo. Gripped by a nicotine craving so strong, he stood outside whilst the rain hammered down around him, turning dips and depressions into puddles and ponds.

'It is, too,' confirmed Paddy. 'What's he doing there? I thought he'd been taken down by the SAS?' Nicci shot him a quizzical look but Monica gave a small flare of the nostril accompanied by a shake of the head, the tiniest of gestures but it told her it wasn't worth pursuing an explanation. Paddy's imagination had got itself overexcited, leading to him blurt: 'Does that mean he's a fugitive? Has there been a jailbreak?'

As so often happens, and still no-one knows why, the rain suddenly stopped. It was as if someone had turned off the taps in the sky with a firm twist: one second the sky was grey and the water fell, the next the world was warmed with sunlight bathed in a blue sky. Seeing his opportunity, Paddy leapt from the car and ran towards the Visitors' Centre hollering Pete's name all the way.

Nicci turned to Monica in utter disbelief, saying 'What on earth is he doing now?' but Monica didn't answer. Instead, they watched on. Paddy, in long wide-legged strides, tiptoed and pirouetted around the puddles before reaching Pete. They shook hands like long-lost friends. Paddy must have asked a question because Pete launched into an animated monologue. Pete was one of those people that use their cigarette as a pointer when they speak; its glowing red end flitted about like a kamikaze firefly on a joyride. When he stopped speaking his arms fell to his side, the cigarette made one last swift trip to the lips and then the butt was flicked down to the nearest puddle. Pete rapped his knuckles against the fire door. It popped open, he entered through, and it closed. Paddy looked across, he saw Monica and Nicci watching and with an exaggerated scooping gesture he beckoned them over. Monica released the door handle and began to exit the car, only to notice Nicci hadn't moved.

'You go, I'll catch up,' said Nicci, 'I need to make a quick call, find out what's going on.'

SEVERAL MINUTES HAD PASSED: nothing had happened. The female police officer in the corner shuffled from foot to foot to chase away the onsetting stiffness. The tufty-eared solicitor fiddled with his fountain pen: screw on, unscrew off, screw on, unscrew off. Monica slowed her breathing, and kept her eyes closed. Internally she searched for her happy place, but it was nowhere to be found, just a Chernobyl-sized hole smouldering gently amidst the rubble.

'IT WASN'T HIM, MON.' Paddy was breathless in his delivery, desperate to tell her everything he'd found out. He shuffled across to offer her more shelter under the eaves, then continued his rapid delivery. 'The police came for him mob-handed, took him in under armed guard and everything. But had to let him go in under an hour.'

Monica was perplexed, but also wanted Paddy to draw a breath before he collapsed so she interrupted him. 'Why? Everything pointed to Pete being the guilty party.'

'I know. And the funny thing is, he agreed. But he had a rock-solid alibi.'

Inwardly Monica cursed, but her curiosity had the better of her. She was so convinced of Pete's guilt she was having trouble comprehending what had just happened. She urged Paddy to explain, then immediately regretted it after hearing a little too graphically about a middle-aged man's doctor's appointment for a middle-aged man's condition involving the aforesaid middle-aged man bending over to touch his toes whilst his doctor snapped on a rubber glove.

Blinking away the images it seared in her mind, Monica tried to bring Paddy back to their own predicament. 'But ... where's that leave us now?'

'I've no idea, Mon, but I'm getting cold out here. Fancy a hot chocolate to warm you up?' Paddy, copying what he'd seen Pete do, gave a couple of hefty thumps against the fire exit. It popped open almost immediately. Paddy swung it open to its full extent. 'I'm going inside. Coming?' Monica nodded and followed him through.

They emerged in the back-of-house prep area to the café. Alison, the large lady in an apron, waited inside the doorway. She shot a suspicious look at Monica as if to say, 'Who are you? Why are you doing the friends and family knock?' then she noticed Paddy and let the animosity go: *I wouldn't mind being friends with this guy.* She made for the door, deliberately reaching across Paddy, as well as up and down Paddy, to do so. Grabbing the release bar, she firmly closed the door and shot the bolts back into place. Alison gave the door an inquiring shake to check it was properly shut, then turned to Monica.

'Are you with my dad?' Alison asked Monica, gesturing with a flick of the chin. The café was still full to bursting with customers sheltering from the rain, not a spare seat in the house, but Monica followed the gesture over to Pete, who had taken a stool behind the serving counter; Paddy had already gone across to join him.

'Yes, I am ... we are,' lied Monica.

'Did you hear his good news?'

'I did, yes, Paddy told me,' replied Monica. 'You must be pleased.'

'We certainly are,' the relief came loud and clear through Alison's demeanour, but in less than a heartbeat her face hardened and her mood darkened. 'If I ever find out who grassed and spread lies about my Dad, I'll rip their face off, you hear me? They'll wish they'd never been born.'

'Yeah,' Monica hoped she sounded believable, then added for a bit of flourish and distancing, 'Yeah, the idiots, they'll be sorry!'

'Hey Monica, come over here,' Paddy called across the room, summoning her. Inwardly Monica thanked him for saving her from Alison's aggressive staring; she gave a meek smile to Alison and scurried over.

Paddy greeted Monica with a smile. 'One bright thing to come out of today's fiasco, Mon,' he said, his arm draped over Pete's shoulder, 'is I'm in the clear, isn't that right Pete?'

Pete looked a little abashed and ashamed; he dipped his head in a guilty nod. Monica flashed a quizzical look, flicking her eyebrows up in expectation of an explanation.

Paddy obliged. 'So I was talking to Pete about getting hauled in by the cops, and I said to be fair it did look a bit suspicious what with him suddenly appearing and then shooting off again so fast.'

'At the car park, you mean?' replied Monica seeking clarification.

'That's right. I said to Pete, what were you doing coming down here in your best clothes and your camper van, then speeding off almost straight away, and Pete said ...'

Taking this as his cue, Pete continued the thread, 'I wanted to clear Boot Camp Dan's stuff out of our birdwatching hide.'

Monica looked at both men as if they were insane. 'I don't understand?'

Paddy took a breath, then began, 'Remember I said Boot Camp Dan kept accusing me of pinching his stuff? And I kept insisting to everyone it wasn't me? Well—'

'It was me,' blurted Pete. 'I was annoyed at him getting us moved off our space then one morning I saw he'd laid out his cones for a training session, so I picked them up, just to be a nuisance. I didn't know what to do with them, I didn't want to chuck them in the river and pollute the wildlife, so I stashed them in our hide. The next day, he laid out some more, I took them. And then it became a habit, I suppose. Just a bit of mischief and nonsense. Anyway Alison called me as I was leaving the consultant's to say he'd been murdered and the police were swarming the place, so I figured I'd better come down and get rid of them quick. But then you lot all got in my face and I panicked and decided to go before I attracted too much attention.'

'See, I told you it wasn't me,' beamed a vindicated Paddy.

'I told the police about it,' continued Pete, ignoring Paddy, 'and they didn't seem that bothered. I guess because he's got no use for them now, what with him being dead and all. But that's why I came down in a hurry that day. Maybe I can return his gear to his family, maybe they'll have a use for it.' Pete's voice trailed off in regret and self-recrimination. Paddy beamed triumphantly; his name cleared against petty nonsense.

'WON'T BE LONG NOW,' chirruped the female police officer in the corner, breaking the silence. Yet more minutes had passed, the lawyer had grown tired of fiddling with his fountain pen and now polished his glasses with a crumpled tissue he'd pulled from his jacket pocket. Monica sighed and stared at the door.

THE RAIN HAD STOPPED. The café crowd began to thin out. Drinks were finished and baked goods consumed, arms slid into sleeves and coats returned to shoulders. Hats were replanted. In a slow but steady flow they drifted out of the café, all muttering between themselves: *I don't know what's going on with the weather this year, I wish it'd make its mind up.*

The café, previously bursting at the seams, was now two thirds empty, but still had enough occupied tables and prams blocking aisles to make the police officers' approach awkward. The young lad, Caffrey, resembled a baby deer; with long gangly steps he attempted to pick out a path. Behind him, the old malingerer Perkins followed in a bad mood. Several handbags got trodden on and a rucksack went flying across the room, hoofed in the air by an accidental kick. Or at least he later claimed it was accidental, because in truth his patience threshold was as low as his footsteps.

From their stools behind the counter, they watched the two policemen tackle the obstacle course with the grace and agility of punch-drunk clowns. Eventually they reached the counter and gripped the edges of it, as if it rode the roughest seas.

'Good morning, gentlemen,' Alison greeted them, holding back a laugh. 'What can I get for you.'

Caffrey waited for his senior partner to speak, but after a long pause it became apparent Perkins hadn't got his breath back from his exertions and possibly wouldn't for some time yet. Caffrey looked at the two women behind the counter, and enquired, 'Monica Minton?' The small dark-haired lady raised her hand. 'Monica Minton. If you could come with us please, we'd like to speak with you back at the station.'

'What? Why?' demanded Paddy, leaping to her defence.

'To answer questions regarding the murder of Boot Camp Dan,' came a loud commanding voice from the other end of the room. Monica, Paddy, Alison and every single person in the café turned to see Detective Constable Sharma framed in the entranceway. 'Come with us please, otherwise the officers have instructions to arrest you.'

CHAPTER **EIGHTEEN**

ONLY FOLLOWING ORDERS! Nicci Sharma hated herself for even considering the phrase, never mind using it, but that was exactly what she was forced into.

She'd never seen happy-go-lucky-laid-back Paddy so incensed before. His violet eyes darkened and his lips tightened watching Perkins and Caffrey lead Monica away. From being in a place of such promise, she knew right now he regarded her as the enemy and she worried he always would. *Only obeying orders*, that phrase again.

Nicci wanted to connect with the Paddy she knew and make him think rationally. 'I had no choice, Paddy,' she pleaded. 'The instruction came through on the radio after you left the car. Canning's convinced Monica is hiding something.'

Paddy's snort of derision was all that was needed to convey his disagreement and displeasure, but he couldn't help asking, 'Hiding what?'

'Well, that's what he seems determined to find out. He's convinced she put forward such a comprehensive case for it to be Pete that it must've been an elaborate ruse to deflect attention away from her.'

'Why's he convinced it was her? You said it was an anonymous call.'

'Because,' replied Nicci, 'despite it coming through on an unregistered, untraceable phone your sister introduced herself at the start of the call.'

It was true; regardless of using her best endeavours to make an anonymous tip-off Monica found her corporate training too ingrained, and hard-wired impulses kicked in automatically the moment her call connected to Canning's voicemail: *Mr Canning, this Monica Minton, it's eleven forty-three and I have some information for you ...*

Paddy shook his head, unable to believe his sister had been so naïve but at the same time believing it entirely. However, he was without any shadow of a doubt convinced Canning had got this course of action wrong, and taking Monica in was a grave miscarriage of justice.

Nicci's snort of derision that was all that needed to convey her displeasure: you're preaching to the converted, Paddy. Yet again, that phrase, *only obeying orders.*

'I actually did you both a favour. A big one,' added Nicci. 'Canning was all for sending the tactical firearm squad in again, but I persuaded him it wasn't necessary. And doing it my way, Paddy, she's not been arrested.'

'The difference being?'

'The difference being it makes things a whole less complicated for her.'

FUNNILY ENOUGH, THINGS didn't feel any less complicated for Monica Minton waiting in a drab cuboid room. The door opened. Canning entered. Behind her she sensed the female police officer stiffen. Beside her the drowsy, tufty-eared solicitor sat up with a jolt.

Monica's corporate instincts kicked in. Years of meetings, every single day, some difficult, some contentious; she was used to this arena and as with any formal meeting she rose to her feet, made a smile and extended a hand to shake. Canning, slightly discombobulated by this, reverted to his previous life selling mortgages and pensions, and found himself warmly shaking hands and grinning a salesman's smile. Conscious of the sniggers around him, most notably DC Sharma who'd followed him in to join the interview, he dropped hands and the smile dissolved in favour of a scowl. 'So, Monica Minton, I've got a bone to pick with you.'

'And what would that be, Mr Canning?'

A vein throbbed at Canning's temple, 'How about that fools' errand of an arrest, for a start? Do you know how many police resources you wasted today?'

'When was this, sir?' DC Sharma carried a convincing tone of surprise in her query. 'I was only aware of your operation. Was there another operation today?'

Monica recognised the importance of the intervention made by Nicci Sharma, and made a point to thank her later. Canning, however, made a point to bawl her out later: *how dare she butt in and interrupt me in front of a suspect.* Nicci Sharma wasn't unduly worried, she knew the rule book better than he did. She knew she could simply deflect his ire by telling him she was protecting him from prejudicing himself in any legal proceedings regarding the anonymity of confidential informants and take comfort in the knowledge that he wouldn't know whether or not she was telling him the truth, and that he was too lazy to find out.

Canning crossed his arms; he gave a harrumph. The vein at his temple throbbed harder, enlarged and darker. Deciding a new approach was required to shake things up a bit, Canning threw out the question, 'I hear you've been getting hate mail? And threatening phone calls?'

The question, delivered with a nasty sneer in his voice, unsettled Monica. A cold, uncomfortable sensation dowsed her; she felt vulnerable. 'That's right,' she replied, her voice barely audible despite the airless still of the room.

'I hear they're accusing you of Boot Camp Dan's murder. Making a lot of noise, I hear.' As he delivered his words, he leant further and further across the table, getting closer and closer to her. 'Maybe they've got a point?'

Sensing the wash of emotions prickling her eyes, Monica turned her face from him.

Thankfully her solicitor had finally found his voice. 'Mr Canning, in this country we are bound by the rules of law, not the baying mob and whoever shouts loudest. My client, a young woman, has been subjected to a horrific campaign of abuse and harassment. Why are you, a senior police officer, adding to this instead of countering it? Is this an instance of the police doing what I believe the newspapers like to call victim-blaming?'

Canning shuffled back, until he was rigid upright in his chair. He didn't like the way this interview had turned: *how did this happen, how come I'm now the one coming under fire?*

The tufty-eared solicitor hadn't finished: 'An intruder ransacked my client's home yesterday, yet you appear to be suggesting she deserved such an attack? Does your superior officer agree with this? Perhaps I need to raise it with the Chief Constable, to confirm whether this is a new police strategy?'

It was at this point Canning realised he'd gambled and lost. He'd thrown a hand grenade of a question out there expecting it to liven up the discussions, only to have it explode in his lap. He still smarted from the last dressing-down he'd had from his guv'nor; the very last thing he needed was for this to reach the ears of high command. Assessing his options, the best solution seemed to be to admit defeat and get out of this claustrophobic little room with as much face saved as possible.

'I'm going to let you go with a warning, Miss Minton—'

The solicitor flashed him a stern schoolteacher's stare over the top of his glasses. 'A warning? For what precisely?'

'I'm going to let you go, Miss Minton,' replied Canning, ignoring the sound of Nicci Sharma's smirk behind his head and the vein drumming inside it, 'but don't think that's it. I'm watching you.'

'I should hope so too,' the solicitor's tone took on a patronising tone, one that put Canning firmly in his place. 'I take it you'll be instructing a police guard outside Miss Minton's house to protect her safety?'

Canning stared at the man, agog. The man hadn't broken eye contact, he was expecting an answer and it was clear he wouldn't drop the matter until he got one. Canning's head spun, unsure whether his authority extended to signing off on twenty-four-hour personal protection but fairly sure it didn't. 'I'm sure that won't be necessary,' he finally stammered.

'Hmm, we'll see,' replied the solicitor, with the clear implication he was going to be a right royal nuisance about it. 'And how is the investigation into Miss Minton's home invasion progressing? What can you tell us?'

Searching for an answer, gears spun inside Canning's head, freewheeling, desperately trying to connect onto something, anything. He'd seen an email come in about it, he was certain of that, but he hadn't bothered reading it, why would he: *who cares about a poxy break-in when I've got a tactical firearms squad and a helicopter to command?* No matter hard he tried he came up dry, he had absolutely nothing to offer. Eventually, he looked back over his shoulder: 'Sharma? Any news?'

Nicci Sharma struggled to keep the glee from her voice: so far her plan to follow Canning's command to the absolute letter was working; sure, it had caused friction between her and Paddy but Canning was exposing himself more and more incompetent as every hour passed. 'The scene of crime team took samples and evidence from Miss Minton's home,' she said, talking directly to the solicitor, ignoring Canning as the irrelevant in the room. 'It's being processed at the moment, and due to her connection to the Boot Camp Dan murder I've managed to expedite it.' Canning nodded sagely as if all was as he'd expected and he was comfortably on top of things. She turned and spoke to Canning, 'I said you'd authorise the funding for fast-tracking it.' Canning coughed his surprise.

Nicci diverted her focus, and now looked at Monica as she spoke, holding eye contact, creating an intimacy across the room. 'We're doing everything we can. The tech team are confident they'll trace the emails and text messages to their originators within the next day or two. Unfortunately, there were no fingerprints found at your home connected with the break-in, whoever it was must've been smart enough to wear gloves, but I've been talking with the Forensic head and she thinks she might have a lead. There were a couple of tiny blood smears around the broken window, she thinks they may have scratched themselves when they reached in to unlock the door. She's hopeful there's enough to analyse and test. If they're in our system we should find out who they are in the next couple of days. So, try to relax, we're doing everything we can.'

'Thank you,' replied Monica.

'Thank you,' echoed the solicitor.

'You're welcome,' replied Canning.

Idiot, thought all present.

CHAPTER **NINETEEN**

IN MONICA'S PREVIOUS LIFE, breakfast had been grab and go: something to be eaten at her desk, purchased from one of the coffee shops between station and office. It'd been very immediate and urgent, always conscious of the clock. Striving to become ever more time-efficient she'd recently begun ordering online: using an app on her phone she'd place her order shortly before she arrived at the station, enabling her to walk at a brisk pace, straight up to the counter of her favourite store, no queueing required, where a freshly brewed coffee and a warm pastry would be waiting for her to pick up and go, barely a second wasted.

Monica hadn't quite got the hang of breakfast under her new regime. Never having had a need before, her cupboards had nothing she liked to eat when starting the new day. Instead, she found the stuff Paddy chose for himself: brightly coloured boxes with cartoon characters, filled with confections masquerading as cereal; the sort that turbo-charges a hyperactive seven-year-old on a day-long sugar rush. Deciding she could do without headaches and heart palpitations, she opted for a slice of dry toast and a small glass of orange juice. She still couldn't quite get her head around the fact that she was watching TV at seven thirty in the morning, that she could have a bath or squeeze in a short run or do some laundry, and still be at work on time. She was finding the adjustment hard. Her corporate mind kept reminding her she'd avoided a ninety-minute commute and therefore there was an extra hour and a half she could be working. However, the Minton mind she shared with Paddy told her to take it easy: *there's nothing you can do until you collect the first batch of dogs at nine, so relax.*

The television annoyed her. The hot topic was something to do with energy prices. Every fifteen minutes they cut to a poor reporter outside a totally dark, closed-up government building. Monica didn't understand why: *she's been out there in the cold and gloom since six o'clock, nobody's in that building and they won't be for another couple of hours, so why does she need to be there? We all know what an office block looks like, why can't you let her talk to you in your nice dry studio? And now you're asking her – yet again – to repeat what she's already told you several times already – oh for god's sake, of course nothing's changed, there's nobody working in there yet, you can see that, just let the poor girl come indoors and warm her bones.*

Monica had had enough. She switched off the TV, gulped down the last of her juice and declared she had things to do; she just hadn't worked out what. Luckily for her, the phone rang.

'HOLD ON A MOMENT, let me put you on speaker so that Paddy can hear.'

Monica barged into Paddy's darkened bedroom, her phone wedged between shoulder and ear. She shook Paddy; with a groan and a few fruity swears he awoke.

'Budge up,' she whispered, nudging him to move. Resistance seemed futile and he obediently slid over. His bleary mind ticked over but hadn't yet reached full running speed. Monica perched on the edge of the bed and lay the phone on the pillow between them: 'Go ahead.'

Nicci Sharma, for it was she calling, began to speak. Her voice came loud and clear through the phone: 'Hi Paddy.'

Now he was awake: lights, camera, action, five-star Paddy was in the room. 'Morning Nicci, how's you this fine morning?'

'All's good with me. You?'

Regretting her initial decision and suddenly feeling like an unwanted guest in her own phone call Monica butted in, 'We're all great, Nicci. So, how can we help you?'

Correctly deciphering Monica's passive-aggressive question, Nicci switched into Detective Constable Sharma mode, and her tone reflected that: 'I'm calling about your complaint of continued telephone and email harassment.'

Monica hadn't had a call or a text or even an email since yesterday morning and part of her had hoped that if she didn't think about it, it'd go away. This unwelcome and unexpected mention churned an ice-cold slurry around Monica's stomach. She didn't know how to respond.

The silence extended a second too long and the awkwardness was recognised by Nicci. 'I have good news for you. Our tech team managed to trace the source to a sole perpetrator: a woman by the name of Pamela Kent, living on the outskirts of Aberdeen. Do you know Mrs Kent?' She waited for Monica to confirm she didn't, then continued, 'I didn't think so. I've spoken with colleagues from Police Scotland who paid her a preliminary visit yesterday. By all accounts she's been living with her elderly mother since her husband ran out on her almost thirty years ago. Their opinion was she's mostly harmless, but had developed a bit of a fixation on Boot Camp Dan in her loneliness. Apparently her ninety-one-year-old mother was furious when she heard what she'd been doing to you and gave her a proper telling-off in front of the police officers and made her promise never to do it again. The officers have arranged to go back later today, subject to instructions from me. I therefore need to ask: how do you want this to proceed?'

If anyone knew Monica, they knew what she'd want done. Monica had always been very disciplined and very regimented in everything; *rules were rules, they were there for a reason and if we all followed them, we'll all get along fine.* Her space and her sanity had been violated, there were rules against it. She opened her mouth to respond but felt Paddy's hand land gently on her forearm. She looked to him. With his eyes fixed on hers, he gave a slow shake of the head: 'She's a confused old lady, Monica, she's said sorry, let it go, please.'

Monica paused, letting the words sink in. 'Please tell Police Scotland we are very grateful to them, and that a caution is sufficient,' were her instructions to Nicci Sharma, but the lifelong sibling rivalry needled at the back of her mind: *I hate it when he's right.*

And so, to punish her brother for making her do the right thing she stood and threw open his curtains. The daylight flooded in, making him squint, and his jeans hit him square in the face. 'Paddy, get dressed. We're going out.'

IT WAS A MINUTE or two before eight when the Mintons reached the Handsome Smoothie, James Doyle's place. The iron gates stayed open to allow through the before-school motorcade of SUVs ferrying little Tarquin to his Mandarin lessons and Jocasta to her harpsichord practice; Monica nipped her small car through before they closed, securing the enclave from outsiders once more.

'I don't know what I'm doing here,' moaned Paddy; he still resented being hauled out of his bed at what he insisted on calling the crack of dawn, despite dawn having long since packed its bags, its work done for another day.

'Because if I'm working, you're working, that's how partnerships work,' replied Monica. 'And besides, I'm worried, what if there are more nut-nuts out there, watching me?' Paddy recognised that as a fair concern but seeing as their entire relationship as siblings involved squabbling, he gave a half-hearted grumble to keep up appearances.

It was too early in the morning for Monica to maintain any pretence of argument and instead tried to give him a gee up. 'Come on, we're here now, sooner we begin sooner we're done.' And upon saying that took herself down the perimeter path around the back of the house, as she did before, to unlock the door and let herself in. Paddy waited under the canopy of the front porch, yawning, stretching and treating himself to a good scratch. By the time she'd opened the front door to him, he was deep in conversation with a man in a red fleece jacket.

'Hey Monica,' he said, turning to face her, 'look, it's Gary.' Monica offered a polite smile but had no idea nor interest who Gary was, or why Paddy was so excited to see him. Thinking himself helpful, Paddy gladly informed her, 'Don't you recognise him? He's Mum's postman.'

Gary nodded a gap-toothed gleeful smile, glad to be noticed for once. 'That's right. I start my round on this side of town working my way across to finish up near where your mum lives. Every day, rain or shine, I begin here between seven thirty and eight, and by the time I get to your mum's road, it's close to eleven.'

Monica, unable to disguise quite how much she found this conversation pointless and boring, was keen to wrap it up and get back to work. 'Got anything for Mr Doyle? We're looking after the house whilst he's away.' Receiving a few slim envelopes and a wine-club pamphlet, she returned into the house. 'Come on, Paddy, work to do.'

UNCLE ALBERT WAS IN a bad mood. He'd rather enjoyed having the house to himself; having the choice to curl up on any seat he fancied without fear of being nudged off, and the prospect of a nice long satisfying claw on the curtains without the risk of being bopped by a rolled-up newspaper was delicious. Now this noisy pair of interlopers had come back to pester him, clumping about with their big feet and big hands and oh, the loud voices, that was the worst. Hearing them squabble and bicker in the entrance hall was unbearable. Uncle Albert slunk upstairs, nudged open a door and found a nice quiet spot under the spare bed to hide.

Monica, on all fours, looked up from under the kitchen table and fixed Paddy with a hard stare. It didn't stop Paddy asking for the third time, 'I said, why can't we just leave a bowl and go?' The hard stare became a lot harder.

'Because we need to see the cat. That's the key part of this job, making sure the pets are alright. Until we see the cat, we're not going anywhere.'

Paddy sighed; he knew she was going to say that. He leaned against the breakfast counter, bored.

Honestly, I don't know what's harder: herding cats or herding Paddy, she thought to herself, crawling into the utility room and rummaging through a coat cupboard.

'Paddy, tell you what, you look upstairs for him, I'll do downstairs. He must be here somewhere.'

AFTER TEN MINUTES of scrabbling around on his hands and knees scouring under beds and wardrobes Paddy spied a pair of sparkling green eyes blink out at him from under the valance: 'Aha, there you are matey.' He enticed Uncle Albert out from under the bed and scooped him up in his arms.

Privately Paddy enjoyed the vibrating sensation through his arms and chest brought about by the purrs of the cat, though he'd never admit that out loud to anyone. The drowsy cat, cradled by Paddy, was almost asleep when they both entered the home office of James Doyle, the Handsome Smoothie. 'What are you doing in here, Mon?'

Sat in the Handsome Smoothie's fancy swivel chair, Monica had an open folder in front of her on the desk. 'Looking for the cat,' she replied in a faraway voice, not lifting her eyes from the folder.

Paddy gently deposited Uncle Albert on an armchair in the corner of the room; it was a smart-looking piece of furniture, no doubt expensive, in an emerald-green velvet. Paddy smiled inwardly, proud of his little bit of mischief: *hope you enjoy trying to get all the white hair off of that, Dodgy Doyle.*

Monica still hadn't shifted her attention from the document before her, so to pass the time Paddy browsed the shelves of James Doyle's office. With indifference, he glanced over a university degree in an ornate frame; a cluster of photographs caught his interest. One showed the Handsome Smoothie at a golfing event, complete with the de-rigueur visor and single white glove; he clutched a silver cup. Another showed him at a circular table with six or seven other men, all dressed in tuxedos and black bow ties, a large cut-glass trophy deliberately posed in the centre of the table to catch the light; some sort of industry awards dinner, Paddy surmised. Paddy leaned forward, scrutinising the images of James Doyle: *there's something about you, I don't know exactly what it is, but I know there's something about you I don't trust.*

'Oh my god!' squealed Monica, snapping Paddy out of his character assassination. She sat bolt upright in the seat, as if something on the page had leapt out to bite her. She held a sheet of stiff white paper in her hand, and from where he stood Paddy could make out a claret-red letterhead across the top.

'What is it, Monica?'

'It's a letter from Herr Geerhart, in Geneva.'

'Geneva? Isn't that where your Smoothie is right now?'

'He's gone to visit his investor; this investor,' replied Monica. She held the document a little higher and shook it for emphasis. 'Probably about this very letter.'

Now Paddy was intrigued. Scooping up Uncle Albert, he sat down in the green velvet chair and let Uncle Albert settle on his lap. With a raised eyebrow, he gestured for Monica to continue. She began to read aloud:

'Dear Mr Doyle, I write on behalf of Herr Geerhart, chief executive and chair of the Geerhart Foundation, regarding the opportunity to participate in the venture capital investment of the fitness brand known as Boot Camp Dan—'

Monica shot daggers from her eyes at Paddy's interruption. It was an involuntary reflex; he couldn't stop himself snorting at the ridiculous thought of his arch-enemy ever becoming a household brand. He raised a finger in apology and beckoned for her to continue.

'On Herr Geerhart's instruction I have conducted our own due diligence into the principal and founder, and regret to inform you that this opportunity does not reconcile with the Geerhart Foundation's ethical investment policy nor guidelines. I therefore confirm, on behalf of Herr Geerhart, that the Geerhart Foundation declines to proceed any further and withdraws from this opportunity.'

Paddy's expression suggested he understood the implications of the letter about as much as Uncle Albert did. Uncle Albert stood, turned in a circle, kneaded Paddy's belly, then curled up for a kip. Paddy meanwhile waited for a translation into layman's language.

'What it means, Paddy, is that James Doyle's lead investor looked into Boot Camp Dan's history themselves, discovered his performance-enhancing-drug disgrace, and pulled out of the deal and ...' Monica squinted at the letter again to be sure, 'James has used a received stamp to record when he got it.' She was quietly impressed, she loved an organised mind and made a mental note to order herself a date stamp when she got home. 'It came the same day as Boot Camp Dan was murdered.'

'Didn't they know beforehand about his dodgy past?'

'No, I don't think so.' Monica flipped back through the folder then stopped and jabbed a finger at a document. 'This is an investment prospectus he'd produced.'

She passed across to Paddy a glossy sheet of paper, the size of a letter but folded in half to create a booklet of four sides, each with colourful graphics and photos. He scanned the text: it all sounded too good to be true, he almost wished he had the money to invest then remembered it was his arch-enemy, now deceased, and the Handsome Smoothie, alive but untrusted. The text made big news of Boot Camp Dan's youth boxing prowess, but at no point did it even hint at his fall from grace.

'Maybe your Smoothie didn't know about it himself?' suggested Paddy, not quite believing he was actually defending him.

'I thought that too,' Monica replied. She flicked further through the folder, stopping almost at the very back of it. 'But look here, right at the very start of his time with Boot Camp Dan, he commissioned a background check into him, it says everything here in black and white.'

'So, he knew but ploughed on regardless, not telling anyone?' Paddy felt vindicated, he knew he'd been right, there was something suspect about the Handsome Smoothie, the whole thing sounded underhand and duplicitous to Paddy.

'Or, you could say he was the better man because of it,' countered Monica. 'He could've decided: so what? Yes, Boot Camp Dan made a bad choice when he was a very young man, not much more than a boy, but he served his punishment so why isn't he entitled to a second chance, why can't he redeem himself?'

Paddy hated it when Monica was right. With a shove, Uncle Albert flew off his lap and a bad-tempered Paddy shuffled in the chair, crossing one knee over the other in a sulky flounce. Uncle Albert fixed him with a green-eyed stare, then sauntered out of the room with his nose held high.

'All this tells us,' she continued, 'Is that James had lost his principal investor, and that they were annoyed that he'd kept what they considered a key fact from them. So, he's now in Geneva on his knees pleading forgiveness in the hope of saving his reputation and his business.'

Paddy's bad mood improved; he liked the idea of Handsome Smoothie grovelling. He brushed a clump of white cat fluff from his jeans and said, 'Well, we've had proof of life, the cat's fine and dandy, let's get out of here.'

HAZEL HUNG ON EVERY WORD Paddy spoke, her attention unwavering. When he'd finished, she fished her notebook out of her bag, and flipped through for a blank page. Pencil poised, she looked up at Paddy and Monica and asked, 'Geerhart? How's that spelt, like it sounds?' and she began scribbling notes. Another rummage in her bag produced a tablet device, and a quick tap brought it to life. She didn't speak again after that, lost in her own little world of screen-surfing and note-taking.

'Eeugh, flowery, yours.' Paddy swapped the Earl Grey with the one beside Monica, then said, 'I don't suppose Doyle will suffer too badly from this. His sort never do.'

'What do you mean by that?' asked Kenton, picking up on the edge to Paddy's tone.

'The Handsome Smoothies of this world. They all get by on charm and smarm, never facing any consequences.'

Monica's expression couldn't hide her disbelief that Paddy, who had coasted through his entire life without ever once needing to make a decision or have a difficult conversation, was talking about facing consequences, but before she could say anything Comedy Tim piped up:

'You know ... I'm not handsome, rich or athletic ... what? You're expecting a "but"?!' he sat back enjoying the reception his line had got; genuine laughs from everyone.

'That's very good,' replied Paddy, 'You could use that in your act. Is that one of your jokes?'

Comedy Tim's face fell, and began to redden, his voice dropped to little more than a whisper. 'No. It's a very old pub gag.'

'Oh, well, it's very good all the same. Perhaps you can still use it in your routines,' suggested Monica, 'That reminds me, Paddy said you went for a big audition for a radio show, did you ever hear any more about that?'

Comedy Tim shook his head, his voice gone entirely, his face reddened further, and he reached for his phone. From the edge of her vision, she caught Paddy giving her silent signals to stop talking and she let the matter drop for fear of embarrassing him further.

Kenton shifted his weight in his seat, 'You've still not explained what you meant Paddy, why won't James Doyle suffer from his bad deal?'

'Insurance,' Paddy stated with great confidence. 'He was insured up the wazoo, he'll get paid out, he'll be fine.'

'He took out life insurance on Boot Camp Dan?' asked Tim with the sound of amazement in his voice. 'That can't be right, surely?'

'Tell him, Monica,' Paddy, now way out of his confidence zone, passed the buck so deftly it didn't have chance to slow down.

'Not quite,' Monica advised the group. 'He's got a type of business interruption insurance. It covers him should his deal fall through for reasons unforeseen. It can't just be because he can't reach agreement with the other side or he can't get the money to complete it, it has to be a genuine unforeseen catastrophe that renders the deal completely impossible to complete. And given that Boot Camp Dan, the man, was the deal then he'd have a pretty strong case that they'd have to honour his claim.'

Kenton gave a soft whistle of astonishment. 'So he'd get all his money back?'

Monica confirmed he would.

'Even those costs he hasn't actually paid out yet, his ...' Tim's question withered away as he struggled and eventually gave up trying to think of the right word.

'Accruals?' Monica prompted, and Tim clicked his fingers in recognition. 'Usually, yes. If he can prove they are genuine business costs expended in the course of this deal then yes he can. Think about it, anything bought on a credit card, it'd be logged as a cost even though he wouldn't have had to actually pay for it until a month later.'

'Leave it to Mon, she'll find out all the inside gossip,' offered Paddy. 'He's back from Geneva tomorrow afternoon, Monica'll wheedle it all out of him.'

Monica felt both affronted and proud at the same time, and was about to chide Paddy when a loud exclamation came from her left.

'Holy guacamole!'

Hazel's sudden outburst got everyone's attention. They all fell silent and turned their attention to her. Knowing she had a captive audience primed and waiting, she flipped her tablet around, showing them the screen; a wizened old man resembling a walnut in John Lennon glasses looked back at them.

'This debonair young fellow here, this is Ernst Geerhart the third,' said Hazel by way of introduction. 'He comes from a very long line of Swiss bankers. His great-great-grand-uncle established the Geneva bank that is still owned and operated by his family. Apparently, he retired and made way for his son to become the chief executive in 2011, a position he still holds today. But this handsome devil didn't put his feet up and relax, no, instead he established the Geerhart Foundation: a venture capital investment house seeking ethical, green and sustainable start-ups to support. The financial press declared he has the Midas touch on account of the massive successes he's backed; they say where he leads, everyone else desperately follows in his wake, wanting to grab a piece. And if you look just here,' Hazel used finger and thumb to enlarge the screen for all to view, 'you can see he's worth an estimated ...'

A spontaneous and audible 'wow!' came chorus-like from all gathered around the table, and then they fell silent attempting to comprehend such an inconceivable sum,

Monica reflected: no wonder James feels the need to bow and scrape; if you've got the trust of a titan like that you don't let a chancer like Boot Camp Dan squander it for you.

CHAPTER **TWENTY**

IF BREAKFAST WAS CONFUSING TO MONICA, lunchtimes were a whole new level of befuddlement. The very idea of going home for lunch? In the middle of a working day? Her head struggled to get around it in the way an ant does a multi-storey car park. It was all too much. The sight of Paddy plopping himself down on the sofa, pork pie in one hand and remote control in the other, made her head spin in every direction at once: surely lunch is grabbed between meetings, a sushi roll at your desk or a sandwich in a conference?

Paddy, keen to see how England was faring, had hoped to watch some of the cricket but Monica's constant pacing up and down got in the way of the telly. 'Come on, Monica, sit down or go somewhere else.'

Monica heard him and took his advice. She decided to go somewhere else. She didn't know where though. She hovered in the doorway, absent-mindedly chewing on a nail. After finding a minute or so of her lurking more annoying than the pacing, Paddy had had enough. 'What is it, Mon? Something on your mind?'

'How can you just sit here?' The sense of inertia itched at Monica, as if Paddy's sedentariness was infectious. She was restless. 'I just feel like we should be doing something rather than sitting about.'

'I'm only having a quick bite, Mon, give me twenty minutes and then I'm popping up the road to Mrs Pattison's to pick up her fat little podger, Muffin. I thought I'd break him in gently, start with nice slow stroll around the block. Want to join me?'

Monica, about to decline, thought about it and in the absence of anything else to do agreed. 'We're leaving in twenty minutes, okay?'

'Twenty minutes, sure, fine,' agreed Paddy, speaking to Monica but looking at a field in South Africa somewhere. 'And you're out! Well bowled, sir.'

AN HOUR AND QUARTER LATER, Monica had finally chivvied and harangued Paddy out of the front door. He'd managed to cling on to see the last South African batsman out, but eventually needed to admit defeat when his shoes got dropped in his lap and Monica refused to step away from the TV screen.

Mrs Pattison was very pleased to see them again. Paddy got the impression she hadn't seen anyone all day, perhaps longer, and when offered a cup of tea he gratefully accepted knowing it'd cheer the old girl up. A fine china cup and saucer decorated with an old-fashioned floral design was placed in front of him with a rattle. Not wanting to draw attention to the old lady's trembling hands, Paddy gave her a sweet smile that warmed her lonely heart. Perhaps it was being given the chance to talk to someone after enforced loneliness or perhaps it was being in the company of a nice, handsome young man, or perhaps a bit of both, but Mrs Pattison welcomed the chance and before long they were in deep conversation. Monica scowled at Paddy across the surface of the anaemic tea she'd been served, but Paddy didn't care. He rather enjoyed hearing tales of what the High Street looked like back when Mrs Pattison was growing up, and all about the people and families who once lived along the lane they now occupied.

A full forty minutes later, and with the promise to pick up a loaf and a pint of semi-skimmed for her, the Mintons set off on their inaugural walk with the spherical little pug called Muffin. In the same way Mrs Pattison had welcomed respite to her prolonged stay-at-home isolation with a long unstoppable stream of chatter, Muffin over-compensated the sensation of being outside by darting back and forth in all directions, desperate to mark every corner and chase every smell. For a tiny unfit lapdog, he pulled on the line with the strength and determination of a thrashing marlin. When the resistance against her shoulders and upper arms became too tiring, Monica handed the leash over to Paddy for his turn. Instantly Muffin relaxed, and the rod-straight leash slackened; he broke into a happy little waddle alongside Paddy, recognising him as his alpha and leader. Paddy gave a shrug to Monica; half shy, half smug. 'Dogs like me, what can I say?'

IF OBSERVED FROM A SATELLITE, the route they followed was roughly oblong in outline; a simple meander along the pavement for about two kilometres in all, occasionally turning left, so as to bring them back to the start of their route around half an hour later. Paddy led the way, Muffin trotted alongside in a happy little bounce, and Monica brought up the rear carrying a wispy thin plastic bag stretched to breaking point by its meagre contents. A pit-stop at the local convenience store had yielded a carton of milk and a sliced loaf as requested plus a packet of biscuits, which by itself provoked a typical Minton sibling spat: *'Why've you bought biscuits, Paddy?' ... 'She's a nice old dear, I thought I'd give her a treat.' ... 'So you're giving away our profits before we've even started?' ... 'Hey that's the second fire engine I've seen going at full speed, all sirens blazing, I wonder what's happened?' ... 'Stop changing the subject. It's your reckless attitude to money that'll cost this business ...'* and so on. Without declaring a formal truce, one kind of happened by accident in that way they tend to do in petty family squabbles: Paddy and his little pal walked ahead, and a space opened up. Monica hung back slightly. She walked at a slower pace and the separation grew, not a lot, but enough to let the animosity escape and be carried away on the breeze. By the time they were nearing home the three of them walked without speaking, but the mood was happy and equilibrium had been restored to the relationship.

With just her thoughts for company, Monica began to reflect: the sun was shining, the sky was blue, the anonymous abuse and attacks had ceased and all the walking she'd done recently made her feel fitter and more active than she had done for years.

Turning upwards into her lane, commencing the short distance to her front door she declared to herself: *things, for once, are looking good, nothing can possibly go wrong now.*

'Monica,' shouted Paddy back at her, 'Isn't that your car?'

Monica had been daydreaming, lost in her quiet reflection. 'What's that, Paddy?' she answered, not looking up from the pavement directly in front of her.

'The car the fire brigade are putting out. The one that's on fire. It's your car.'

UP AHEAD, LESS THAN a hundred metres, her little car was a blackened, charred mess. She began to run towards it; Paddy followed dragging Muffin behind him. A firefighter directed his hose at the vehicle, blasting it at full power. The water bounced off and channelled down the path. It flowed over the blocked road gulley and continued its journey; gravity drew the water down the gentle fall of the lane until it met the junction with the main road where the levels changed and a pond began to form.

As Monica neared the car, the heat it radiated warmed her face and her feet grew damp, her canvas pumps heavy with water. Before they got any closer another firefighter stepped out between two parked vehicles and blocked their way. 'You can't go any closer, nobody can, it's not safe,' explained the firefighter, his tone placid but firm.

'But that's my car. My house ... oh my god ... is my house okay?'

Monica began to sob. The firefighter cast around for some support; he wasn't there for this. 'It was only one car that was on fire. It didn't spread to any other cars or houses,' he offered, still trying to catch the eye of anyone who could relieve him from this emotional outpouring.

'Monica?' came a voice behind her; a vaguely familiar voice, but one she couldn't visualise. 'Monica?' it called again.

Monica turned in the direction of the voice; she found a young, small woman in jazzy leggings and a sporty zip-up hoodie. Monica studied her face but was unable to hang a name on it.

'Monica, it's me, PC Slater,' she said. 'You probably don't recognise me out of uniform.' Now it all came crashing together: the face, the voice, the name. Monica was frustrated with herself: *I should've known immediately. Even in casual dress and with her hair loose and down, the old me would've known her straight away, the old me was good at networking and making contacts, what's happened to me?*

Monica wavered. Around her, from the edges, it began to grow dark. The darkness edged closer to the centre, like the ending of an old silent movie, until the tiny iris of clarity in the centre of her vision was consumed by the darkness.

MUFFIN SEEMED AGITATED. He wuffed. He wuffed again. Paddy looked around to see what had set Muffin off and discovered his sister collapsed, lifeless on the pavement. A young woman seemingly dressed for the gym knelt beside her shouting desperately into a radio for assistance. The bag had fallen from Monica's grasp when she passed out. It struck the pavement more or less exactly the same time as her head. Milk flowed from the split carton. It mixed with the running water, and splashed a ghostly pale translucence against the kerb stones.

CHAPTER TWENTY ONE

CONSTABLE SLATER WAS BORED. She'd been sitting in the back of the van for close to three hours and was beginning to feel claustrophobic. She'd been paired with her regular partner, Constable Harvey, but he was taking it far too seriously. He'd regularly made it clear he had ambitions for higher things; he wanted to become a detective, maybe even Special Branch. On the rare occasions she'd gone along to the after-work drinks he'd usually stick with the uniforms for one, perhaps two, but then gravitate towards the plain-clothes team, hoping to inveigle his way in with them. Slater felt a little guilty; he was a nice enough guy on the whole, but gossiping about him in text messages to her girlfriend helped pass the time.

Harvey was thrilled. He'd been sitting in the back of the van for close to three hours and was loving every second; his first surveillance operation. *If I do well at this,* he figured, *it could be a feather in my cap, a star in my book, and maybe accelerated promotion*. It was for that reason he took personal control of all the equipment: *Slater should be grateful, look at her, getting paid to play on her phone all morning.*

In an act of the highest self-preservation, Canning had fiddled some budgets and twiddled some rosters and got authorisation to mount a discreet protective watch over

Monica Minton: *that should keep her stroppy lawyer happy.* What Edward Canning lacked in policework, he more than compensated in political cunning. He'd already heard informally that Police Scotland had traced, and were about to deal with, the anonymous harasser; all he needed was to put his name to a twenty-four-hour watch, then he could piggy-back on their success in taking down a vicious cyberbully. Slater's state of tedium and Harvey's state of tension served no other purpose than to make Canning look good, in fact Canning had such little interest in the operation he'd accepted an invitation for a round of golf from the Chief Constable who, knowing Canning's background, was looking for some advice on financial planning, what with his pension coming up soon and all.

It was around the time Canning was strolling between the fourth and fifth hole, extolling the benefits of gilt-edged bonds to the Chief, that the claustrophobia overwhelmed Slater. She remembered a little convenience store not too far away, and reasoning that a break was due, climbed out of the van. The sun was shining, the sky was blue and the air was clear; she breathed it in and felt a giddy headrush of endorphins. Time for a little walk to stretch her legs and clear her head; a short stroll to get herself a bottle of water and maybe a Twix. She opened the passenger door of the van to grab her hoodie, and at the same time asked Harvey if wanted anything from the shop. He didn't respond. She asked again. He didn't respond: *rude*, she thought, *you can take your job seriously but there's always room for manners.*

She decided to give him one final chance to redeem himself and asked for the last time. He hissed at her, flapping a hand behind his back, signalling at her to be quiet.

'Something's happening. There's someone approaching the house.'

Slater peered around the back corner of the van. Expecting a bored door-to-door leaflet dropper going through the motions, she saw a figure moving with purpose. A baseball cap shielded their face but from the set of their shoulders and the way they moved, they were definitely a man, and they were approaching fast. The man paused outside the house: has he seen me, wondered Slater. A shiver of revulsion made her shudder; she knew she'd be in trouble if she'd blown their operation by being spotted. Luckily for Slater the sensation only lasted a second, because the man hadn't spotted her, he'd stopped to search the pockets of his jacket. From where Slater stood, peering around the side of the van, she saw him fiddling impatiently with the cap to a small squarish container: what is that?

HE WAS A MAN IN A HURRY. He'd waited long enough and his staying power had all but run out. The woman and her cretin brother seemed to have no urgency today; when they finally emerged from the house, they only went a few doors up the road. The man was forced to wait some more, and just as he was about to take his chance they suddenly re-emerged; this time the woman was dragged along the street by a greyish blueish creature he assumed was a dog but was much the same size and shape as a pumpkin. The spherical dog led the way, the woman was towed behind it and the brother followed up the rear laughing at them both. Watching them round the corner and disappear from sight, the man knew this was his now-or-never moment. He scanned the environment; from his vantage point he was satisfied there was no traffic and he couldn't see anyone using the footpaths: *this is it, let's get on with it.*

Adopting a quick pace he approached the pretty house with the yellow door, intent to get on with it, and get out again unnoticed. On the periphery of his vision he thought he saw a flash of movement, but when he flicked his eyes across it was gone. He doubted himself, and looked over in that direction, it was somewhere over where an old van stood parked against the kerb: that van's been there all morning and hasn't moved, must be my eyes playing tricks on me. Just to be sure, the man adjusted his baseball cap, pulling the visor lower: *better safe than sorry.*

THE MAN TOOK A backward step from the house, almost butting into the car parked on the road outside: Monica's car. Extending his left arm straight down, the claw-hammer he'd been concealing up his sleeve dropped into his palm. With one fast movement he swung it through the rear passenger window. The soft, crumpled sound of the breaking glass surprised him slightly; it dropped from the point of impact in claggy lumps and tiny cubes, crazed globules hung like stalactites from the framing. Any complacency that may have been swelling due to the tempered safety glass smashing so quietly was quickly chased away by the ear-splitting shriek of the car's alarm, triggered by the intrusion. Snapping back into focus the man pushed his fist through the broken window and upturned the small squarish container he held. A quick flick of the wrist and the container was empty. He withdrew his hand then used it to strike a match. He flicked the lit match through the broken window, and without looking to see it land he'd struck another and thrown it through. Whatever was in the container, it made the back seats of the car combust the moment the match-flame touched it. Within seconds the car was filled with vivid orange flames and cloying black smoke.

Satisfied his work was done, the man stepped away and started quickly in the direction of his own car. He'd covered three paces when a small, plainclothes policewoman clattered into him with the sort of rugby tackle an All Black would be proud of.

THE HOSPITAL WAS LARGE and confusing. Built about ten years ago, it'd been opened by one of the minor Royals; Paddy knew this as he'd walked past the same plaque three times in different directions already. He was finding the signage indecipherable: looking more like a modern art installation, a scribble of coloured lines on the floor mapped out walking routes to different zones with names Paddy could barely pronounce, never mind understand.

'Paddy.' a gentle hand landed on his shoulder. Startled, he turned to find Nicci Sharma. 'I've been looking for you, come on, I'll take you to Monica.'

Nicci expertly led the way, turning left and right through the maze of corridors without once pausing to check the signage. Walking at a pace quicker than his own normal speed, Paddy hurried to keep up with her, and found the exertion made it difficult to walk and talk; thankfully she did the talking for both of them.

'I'm sorry you had to stay behind, Paddy. It must've been hard to see her go off in the ambulance like that.'

SEEING THE CAR ABLAZE, and Monica drop to a dead faint, Paddy panicked about what to do first. A lick of his nose solved that problem for him: the warm wet tongue probing his nostril reminded him he was clutching the fat little pug Muffin. Securing him in the crook of his arm, Paddy jogged the short distance to Mrs Pattison's house at the head of the lane. When there was no response to his ringing on the bell, Muffin got unceremoniously tossed through an open window onto the chintzy sofa beneath with a shout of *'It's only Paddy, Muffin's back. He's had a lovely day out. See you tomorrow, bye.'* Assuming she was inside and she and Muffin were reunited, he made his way back down the lane just in time to see the doors slam on the ambulance, its blue lights illuminate and it pull away.

'Stop, stop,' he called chasing after it, but to no avail; it reached the junction with the main road, the traffic flow paused for it and it drove off without slowing.

Standing bereft in the middle of the street, a friendly female face approached: 'Paddy, remember me, PC Slater?' He did.

'Listen, we're just finishing up with him,' she wafted an arm in the direction of man in a baseball cap. He had his hands cuffed behind his back and the copper with the bulging eyes was manoeuvring him into the back of a police car. 'Give us ten minutes to get him sorted out and then I'll give you a lift to the hospital. How's that?' and true to her word, that's exactly what she did. Within twenty minutes he was deposited at the hospital entrance. She drove away leaving him with a cheery wave and an overwhelming sense of bewilderment as to what to do next.

FOLLOWING NICCI TO a pair of heavy-looking doors, Paddy realised he'd ended up more or less back where he entered the hospital in the first place.

'I saw them arresting someone,' said Paddy. 'Was he the one who set fire to our car?' Nicci confirmed that he was. 'But I thought the Boot Camp Dan threats were behind us now, I thought when you said you'd traced that woman in Scotland it was all over.'

'Yes, he was seen setting fire to your car,' replied Nicci, 'but I can't say any more right now. I need to speak with Monica first. She's through here.' Nicci gave a tilt of her head, gesturing to the double doors. 'You can wait in those seats over there, but I need fifteen minutes to speak with her alone first, is that okay?'

Paddy wasn't listening: his impotence at failing to protect Monica had attached to his frustration at failing to understand a hospital layout, and the resultant simmering anger was beginning to bubble to the surface.

'This all comes down to Boot Camp Dan. Everything was fine until him,' he said, more to himself than anyone. 'We ... Monica's never going to be safe until his killer's found. Where are you with that, eh?'

Nicci Sharma, uncomfortable with the sharpness to his tone and the coldness in his eyes, struggled to find the words.

'I mean, it shouldn't be hard, should it? Who stood to lose the most by Boot Camp Dan staying alive?' He brought his steepled fingers to his lips; a thought had occurred to him. 'Or, turning it on its head, who stood to gain the most by Boot Camp Dan being dead?'

He walked with one extended finger tapping out his thought processes as he paced in tighter and tighter circles, then snapped his fingers. 'I need to go.'

'But what about Monica?'

'Tell her I'll be back soon.'

'Paddy ... but ... where are you going? Paddy?'

CHAPTER **TWENTY TWO**

'I SAID, WE'VE BROUGHT a man in for questioning about the arson attack on your car; his name is Martin Hubbard,' repeated Nicci Sharma. 'Do you know him?'

The very mention of Martin the Ignoramus's full name gave Monica's gullet a bilious burn. Monica, still slightly unsettled, didn't speak; she waited for Nicci to continue.

'I think you do, and I'll tell you why,' began Nicci. 'The reason why it took me a little while to get here was because I was waiting for some test results. You see, we checked his blood and fingerprints. He's the same person that broke into your house.'

Monica had been brought in for observation; initially she'd protested but right now she was grateful for the high-backed chair to sink into whilst her head swam with the news she was hearing.

'From what I gather, Martin Hubbard seems to be saying that the reason we found his blood around your broken window, and indeed why your house got ransacked and your car torched, was purely a "work-related" matter. He seemed confident you'd understand and back him up. Is that the case?'

Monica snorted a laugh of derision and gave her head a gentle wobble: she certainly wouldn't be backing him up and wanted the full weight of the law to come down on him. However, she didn't tell Nicci Sharma that she understood.

ON THE SAME DAY as Boot Camp Dan was killed, and at more or less, give or take, the same time Martin the Ignoramus was summoned to the "Fourteenth".

Monica, a formerly devoted employee of IGR Financial, was fully familiar with the office jargon, she understood the significance of the fourteenth floor: the domain of the senior management, the big boys' lair, large glass office suites looking out across the Thames – million-pound vistas to go with their million-pound salaries. Except Martin hadn't been invited up to admire the view. When Boot Camp Dan was primping himself, Martin the Ignoramus was getting savaged by the business's Chief Executive, the Head of Human Resources and the Head of Legal.

Had Monica known this, she'd have smiled, knowing it served the Ignoramus right; it was about time the bully boy was on the receiving end for once. And if that would have made her smile, the reason behind it would have made her whoop and holler in delight: the reason being her, Monica Minton.

In the days before she quit, Monica had heard whispers on the office gossip grapevine that Martin the Ignoramus had fallen foul of the senior leaders. The operational director's assistant had confided over a few glasses of prosecco one evening that, '*Martin's had his card marked. That report he did for Project Pharaoh was a load of old tosh.*' Monica chose not to respond. She'd worked on the Project Pharaoh report, in fact she did all the work on it – fully in accordance with the brief given to her by Martin, but it was all own her work nonetheless. Ordinarily she'd feel defensive but seeing as she could still feel the bruising from his elbows when he barged her out the way in his quest for glory, she was happy to let him swing for it.

'A waste of paper and ink apparently, that's what I heard,' added her source. 'It caused quite the controversy on the fourteenth.'

But that was nothing compared to the controversy she'd since caused. The Head of Legal wanted to hear it for herself from the lips of Martin the Ignoramus: 'What were her exact words?'

Martin resembled a stunned bullock yet again; it was becoming quite the look for him: his eyes rolled and his fat tongue lolled from the side of his mouth. Words weren't coming, partly because he'd been put on the spot and struggled to understand what was happening, but mainly because he'd never had any respect for Monica and hadn't listened to her most of the time, even more so when she'd had her *"hysterical girly hissy fit"*, as he so gallantly described the incident to his gaggle of fellow pale stale male public schoolboys in the pub after work; they brayed and hooted, celebrating their misogyny and privilege.

'Shall I remind you?' offered the Head of Legal. She may have been a whip-smart ferocious lawyer in one of the top seats of the business but first and foremost she was a woman; she'd experienced the prehistoric and toxic attitudes of Martin and his ilk all throughout her career. She took this kind of incident seriously, and to a degree, personally. She'd done her research. Peering through the thin frameless glasses perched at the end of her nose, she glanced down at the statements in front of her. 'It appears Miss Minton didn't go quietly, and made sure everyone heard her, so I'm surprised you don't seem to remember. I'm told her actual words were: "*You'll be hearing from my lawyers. Workplace bullying. Constructive dismissal.*" Do you remember now?'

Martin the Ignoramus stammered and blustered. He couldn't form a coherent sentence or a plausible excuse; not that it would have done him any good, because it hadn't taken long for those threats to reach the ears of Legal and Human Resources. The Head of Legal glanced again at her paperwork and fanned out the pages; a subtle gesture designed to shock him how many emails and witness statements she'd gathered. The fact she had so many, and given so readily, suggested to her that Martin wasn't particularly popular on the ninth floor, giving credence to the business's concerns and her own suspicions.

Monica's threats may have set some alarm bells ringing; however, the true situation was that she'd totally forgotten she'd made them. Since being manhandled out of the building in the heat of fury and indignation, so much had happened to Monica that she hadn't given it much thought; she certainly hadn't taken it any further.

Nonetheless, the Head of Legal took it seriously. As a lawyer she wanted the business fully prepared to react to any claim brought against it, but as a woman she wanted to make a statement to Martin and his kind that their outdated attitudes and behaviours would no longer be tolerated. If only Monica had known of Martin's humiliating telling-off, she would have felt vindicated, as if she for once had the upper hand.

The Chief Executive, a smart and capable man in his early forties, was in agreement; he came from the new wave of inclusive and inspirational management practice, he wore a suit but never a tie as if to say *'Hey, I'm professional but I'm no corporate robot, I'm one of you guys,'* and he fully supported the Head of Legal's stance. He also saw the wider commercial picture and recognised the bad stain a claim such as this could have on the business's reputation and share value. He was a gently spoken, well-mannered man but he wasn't afraid of difficult conversations and in simple, unemotional language told Martin that he needed to get the matter settled, and in double quick time. He stroked his neatly razored beard and as an added incentive warned Martin that his performance-related pay now depended on it: 'The firm doesn't want any bad press. This is now your number one priority. If you can't make your dispute with Monica Minton go away, there will be no bonus.'

The Chief Executive was a sensible and intelligent man. He wasn't a gangster or a spymaster. The Chief Executive thought he'd been clear and plain in his instruction to resolve the dispute; the Head of Legal and the Head of HR understood exactly what his instruction was, and all present expected Martin the Ignoramus to understand too. They expected Martin to use the same diplomatic, professional methods they themselves would: speak with her, apologise to her, offer her a severance package, even give her her old job back if that's what she wanted. As far as the Chief Executive was concerned, he'd been firm but clear, there was no possibility of misinterpretation. However, he hadn't factored that he was talking to an ignoramus.

A FAVOURITE NUGGET of gossip around the office was that Martin had not so long ago married a very demanding woman over twenty-five years his junior, who'd made it very obvious she regarded the whole thing as a business transaction. Monica empathised with her; if, God forbid, she ever married a man like Martin she'd expect to be heavily recompensed for it too. The prospect of costing him his mega-buck bonus would have been delicious to

Monica; it would certainly make for an interesting conversation at Chateau Ignoramus when he had to tell his trophy wife the money had run out.

Martin may have been an ignoramus, but he wasn't stupid: he knew he was punching above his weight. He knew the only reason why a woman young enough to be his daughter had married him and more significantly he knew what kept her there. Martin knew that if he had to tell her the bonus wasn't coming – the bonus she'd already spent – she'd be gone in a flash. If there was no new Range Rover coming for Laurel, then Laurel would be leaving in the old one, taking him via the cleaners for a full rinsing.

Martin couldn't risk that. He'd be ruined. He was barely solvent as it was; the divorce had cost him a fortune, there was no way he could afford another one. The first Mrs Ignoramus had been a kind and well-meaning, plain and undemanding woman called Wendy. They'd met at university and she'd graciously given up her ambitions of a career in order to support him in his. Wendy bore Martin children, and Martin bore Wendy rigid. Wendy did her best to instil her own values in their two sons rather than his, which she privately found quite embarrassing. So far, they were pretty nice kids and Wendy was proud that they'd soon become kind, well-meaning young men. Wendy was also proud, although she'd never admit it out loud, that they thought their father ridiculous for his mid-life crisis trophy bride and stood by their mother in solidarity. Martin was shocked to find the meek, quiet woman he'd married actually had a spine of steel; Wendy had fought him through the courts and didn't back down on a single thing. She'd won the house, the car, the savings and the boys – not that he'd put much of a fight up for them; their attitudes towards him were loud and clear. Amongst the many things Martin found unfair, and there were a great many, he especially resented the court ordering him to pay ongoing school fees for a pair of ingrates that hadn't so much as uttered a single word to him in over three years. Nonetheless, the boys were doing well at school, the eldest had secured his first-choice university and they were happy with their new lives. Wendy, the former Mrs Ignoramus, had slipped her shackles and reverted to her maiden name; she'd recently fulfilled her long-postponed dream by qualifying as a primary school teacher. Every morning at the start of every day, she never failed to find happiness in the sing-song chant of the children's voices greeting her in unison, 'Good morning, Miss Lamb.'

Martin the Ignoramus didn't go in for introspection, but if he ever stopped to self-reflect, would he say he was happy with his new life? The divorce had wiped him out: savings, investments, pensions, the lot – all gone. His ex-wife took the family home: a tidy, comfortable semi on a leafy, desirable street in South Croydon. Barely letting the ink dry on the documents, Wendy had promptly sold it, claiming it was time to downsize as the boys were almost adults and she didn't need a big family home for just herself. She now lived mortgage-free in a small but attractive new-build on a modern development a mile or two down the road from the old house, keeping the boys close to their friends and schools. Martin, on the other hand, needed to refinance: *a ninety-five per cent mortgage, at my age, so much for early retirement, I'll be working until I'm eighty.*

The new Mrs Ignoramus wanted a four-bedroom mini mansion in an exclusive gated cul-de-sac, and a brand-new Range Rover Sport; a twelve-year-old people carrier may have satisfied the previous Mrs Ignoramus but it simply wouldn't do for the current. As for holidays, Martin's eyes were opened to the wonders of Dubai and the Maldives: *camping, in this country, are you insane Martin, do you know how much my nails cost?* Sadly for Martin he did, and had the bank statements to prove it. The prospect of losing his substantial bonus, and possibly even his job, was overwhelming: Martin knew he needed to take matters into his own hands and get ahead of it.

Martin had bullied an underling in the firm's IT computer service team into handing over Monica's log-in details to her work account. He claimed it was business critical and dropped a few threats to the young techie's career prospects, for good measure. Once in, Martin was convinced he'd find some dirt; something he could use, some shameful posting or inappropriate photo he could use to bargain his way out of trouble. He'd rehearsed it in his head, fancying himself a real-life Tony Soprano: '*If you don't want this getting out, if you don't want to be cancelled and you ever want to work again, then you forget all about me and drop whatever it is you're planning. Comprendez?*'

For several evenings, Martin pored over Monica's entire online history: every email sent and every internet page she'd ever visited. Much to his annoyance he discovered her to be the model employee. Everything was strictly corporate and within company policy, unlike his own internet and email usage which was totally non-compliant and could possibly even be deemed illegal in several countries should law enforcement ever have reason to take a look. Martin paused for thought: *wasn't that how they caught that has-been celebrity, by going through his hard drive? Nah, everything'll be fine*, he convinced himself and poured another drink.

Always a very detail-obsessed person since an early age, one of Monica's talents was her ability to compartmentalise: work phone and work computer for work stuff, personal phone and personal computer for personal stuff. If Martin had ever bothered to pay attention at staff conferences instead of messing around in the back row with his cronies he'd have known it was a company diktat; everyone was meant to behave that way, unlike Martin, whose work computer was a hate crime waiting to happen.

Frustrated that he couldn't yield anything of any use against Monica from her work computer he'd resorted to watching her. He'd easily got her home address from the payroll department, again by abusing his authority with casual threats and intimidation. He'd spent a couple of mornings parked near to her house, watching her come and go, usually with a young man. At first he'd assumed it was a boyfriend, but when a gossipy neighbour asked him why he was watching the street, in a surprising quickness of thought Martin pretended to be a house-hunter new to the area looking for a nice place to live. The gossipy neighbour informed him she was the chair of the residents' group and was delighted to download on to him a history of the street, eventually revealing that the occupants of the house with the bright yellow door were brother and sister. More frustration for Martin, it put an end to any idea of lewd romantic scandal that could be leverage. Also, the brother looked quite big and strong, putting him off the idea of any face-to-face confrontation, he didn't want matey joining in.

As the days passed, Martin's frustration grew and his patience diminished. The Chief Executive, phoning to remind him resolution was a matter of urgency, didn't help ease his anxiety either. The Chief Exec decided to call one morning when Martin was sitting, waiting, outside her house. By sheer stroke of coincidence, just as he was fobbing off the Chief Exec with false assurances that all was in hand, she and the brother left the house. Martin tailed them all across town, right up to the door of Irving, Pickering and Smith: Solicitors. That was it! Martin knew he was out of time: *if she's in there right now discussing her claim with a lawyer, it'll be landing in the Head of Legal's in-box tomorrow morning, I need to do something now.*

Making sure he wasn't seen, Martin scurried down the back alley to the lane. Picking up a handy lump of brick found lying around he hurled it with all his might through the kitchen window of Monica's house. Letting himself in, he immediately found her laptop computer open on the table: *password protected, bah!* Trying a few obvious ideas and failing, he set about looking around the small but cluttered work station she'd set up in her kitchen, searching for anything that might give a clue to her password. He found nothing. The laptop splintered into a thousand shards under the ferocity of his frustration. Later he tried justifying it to himself: *if she had been keeping any notes about me, they're destroyed now*. Seeing piles of paper, and stacks of folders on the bookcase, he quickly flicked through them, scattering the pages in a blizzard of paper. He found nothing about him, or any documentation relating to an employment tribunal. The sound of a key snicking into its lock froze him to the spot; any thoughts of hunting elsewhere in the small house promptly banished. Time was up. He slipped back out the kitchen door and down the back alley, putting as much distance between himself and Monica's house as quickly as he could. Failing to hold back a smug grin, he peeled off his gardening gloves, emitting a little chuckle as he did so: the gloves were a smart move, Martin, you've got away with that big lad, he thought to himself, whilst giving a quick rub to soothe the scratch on his wrist.

'HE SAYS IT WAS a work-related matter, and you'd understand?' repeated Nicci Sharma, looking for a response from Monica.

'I don't work for him,' replied Monica, 'I work for *We Sit Pets.*'

'In that case, I need to know, do you wish to press charges against him?' Nicci had her own tale to tell when it came to persecution and harassment from the pale stale male brigade, and struggled to hold back her smile when she received confirmation. 'Good. Leave it to me.'

The relief that washed through Monica unleashed emotions she didn't realise she'd been suppressing; the ordeal of feeling a victim in her own home was over. She wanted to cry but she also wanted to laugh. She needed someone to hold her, and looked around her with sharp surprise: 'Where's Paddy?'

Nicci turned away from the uniformed officer she'd been speaking with, returning her attention to Monica and advised, 'He said he needed to carry out his duty.'

'His duty?'

'That was his exact words,' answered Nicci Sharma. 'He said he needed to go and feed a cat, that it was his duty, he said he was doing it for you.'

'Feed a cat?' repeated Monica; as far as she was aware they only had the care of one cat on their books presently: Uncle Albert. Why would he go to feed him when James Doyle was due back from Geneva this afternoon? Like the myriad of cogs tumbling and turning in a magnificent old bank vault, suddenly everything slotted into place and unlocked the door. 'He's gone to confront James Doyle. James is the killer.'

CHAPTER **TWENTY THREE**

PADDY CARRIED HIS PHONE, headphones and a bottle of water in a plastic bag. It'd taken him two buses and a ten-minute walk to get to James Doyle's house. A minicab would have been a lot quicker, but they don't work for free.

A chill had descended; the daylight was fading and the evening was itching to get involved. A low setting sun hung behind Paddy's shoulder as he approached the entrance to James Doyle's cul-de-sac; the black wrought iron gates were firmly closed. A push-pad with a voice-box stood against the kerb, a couple of metres in front of the gates. Paddy briefly considered pressing a number at random and telling whoever answered that he had a delivery for them, but then worried it'd look a bit odd if they were watching the camera pointing straight at him: a delivery driver without a vehicle or a package, that'd get the neighbourhood watch twitching. As luck would have it, he spotted the narrow pedestrian gate on the opposite pavement, and realised that was the better option. He gave it a cautious nudge, and as hoped, it swung open; left unlocked for the postman and other essential daily visitors to the big houses on the hill.

Paddy followed the lazy gentle curve of the footpath rising to the contour of the hill. He didn't want to attract any attention; should anyone happen to look out of the window, there goes just another ordinary forgettable guy:

he didn't walk slowly as if scoping out a burglary and didn't walk quickly as if on a mission, he was just someone with somewhere to go, no big deal.

The daylight faded further, triggering the sensors on the street lamps; soft buttery puddles of light fell on the tarmac. Paddy slowed as he neared James Doyle's place. He recognised the car on the driveway without needing to see the registration; the full-length scrape along its flank made it instantly identifiable. Monica was emphatic that the Handsome Smoothie wouldn't be home before seven, but there was his car. James Doyle was home already; *Smoothie must have got an earlier flight*, concluded Paddy correctly.

Paddy paused: *have I made a bad choice coming here?* He'd stopped a couple of houses down from Chez Smoothie, nobody could yet connect him to James Doyle. There was still time to change his mind and go home. Paddy swept his gaze back behind him: there wasn't anyone watching from any windows as far as he could see, in fact there was nothing on the street, no people no traffic, nothing, apart from a crappy old Peugeot parked with two wheels on the pavement. It looked out of place amongst the fleet of shiny, polished SUVs adorning the driveways. It must be a cleaner or a nanny working late, thought Paddy, then forgot about it, his mind in turmoil: *stay or go?*

THE HORIZON TOOK ON the colour of a fresh bruise: purples mixed with greys mixed with yellows. The dwindling natural light gave way to the artificial and it became clear to see which houses were occupied, their windows lit from within, bright oblongs cast out across the lawns. The Handsome Smoothie's was no different, three windows across the ground floor illuminated. Shadows moved across the one Paddy remembered from his previous visit to be the home office: someone was at home.

Injustice at Monica's plight reacted with impulse, spurring Paddy to cross the remaining short distance to Doyle's place. With every step, his confidence rose to keep up with his rising level of indignation. He'd worked it all out. It was all so obvious. Paddy prided himself on his instincts; he was a great believer in first impressions, he'd taken against James Doyle from the very get-go. He didn't know why, but there was something he couldn't quite put his finger on. Outsiders may have thought Paddy's suspicions were borne of jealousy; an antagonism towards someone equally as handsome and charming, but with a purpose and an objective to their life and now reaping the success of their dedication. Paddy, of course, would disagree; he just didn't like him, it was as simple as that, and he'd point out the dogs didn't like him either and dogs, as everyone knows, are the best judges of character. Paddy had never been more certain: James Doyle the Handsome Smoothie was a wrong 'un, and Paddy was going to confront him.

On the driveway, the metallic pings and tings coming from the Mercedes' engine as it cooled suggested that it had been driven hard and driven fast, and that the Smoothie hadn't been home long, perhaps only a few minutes. *Good*, thought Paddy, *he'll be tired, unsettled and confused, he'll be easier to confront.* However, Paddy found the closer he got to the stone pillars of the portico entrance, the more his confidence dissolved, as if he'd sprung a leak and it escaped on the air leaving a cold empty space where there was once the courage of a lion. His crisis of confidence had distracted him, it wasn't until he was virtually upon it that he realised the door was open; not by much, just half an inch or so, as if he'd been expected and they'd left it on the latch for him.

Paddy's inner voice began to question the situation: *He couldn't have seen me coming, he can't have been expecting me?*

Lingering on the doorstep, he heard the scream.

HE'D BEEN MULLING: *press the doorbell or go straight in?* Polite Paddy said the correct thing was to ring the bell, Power Paddy said to barge in and use the element of surprise to his advantage, and Prudent Paddy said perhaps the compromise would be to ring the bell to announce his arrival and step through before Smoothie had a chance to react.

The scream came from deep within the house, snapping him from his procrastination. It wasn't a high-pitched horror movie scream. This was guttural, it was scared, and it was desperate for survival.

CHAPTER **TWENTY FOUR**

AWARE OF THE MAN coming fast up behind him, Paddy spun around and hurled a book straight into his face, then dropped to the ground, hitting the carpet hard. The hammer ripped through the empty air where his head had been a half-second earlier. Things were not going as planned.

Five minutes earlier:
Running without releasing it, Paddy threw open the door and followed the direction of the scream. It took him to the room given over to a home office that'd he'd been in previously with Monica. He remembered it as small but with a neat professional look about it; today it was anything but. Papers lay scattered across all surfaces. Bookcases, previously glass fronted, gaped open with jagged shards embedded in the frames, the panes now a thousand million splinters across the floor. A computer screen lay in a broken heap against the skirting board; above, a blackish scrape smudged the decorations at the point of impact when it struck the wall with force.

Standing at the threshold, Paddy surveyed the wreckage, trying to comprehend what had been going on when a weak, frightened voice snapped his head around in urgent surprise. 'Help me,' it pleaded.

James Doyle, the Handsome Smoothie, didn't look so handsome: blood trailed from his nose, across his chin onto his shirt collar and his right eye had started to close under a fresh and painful-looking swelling. His shirt gaped open, exposing flesh, buttons lost in a tussle. He cowered in a corner, on the floor, beside the green velvet armchair now upturned. A figure stood astride him, a claw hammer raised above their head. From Paddy's perspective it was impossible to distinguish anything about them: they had their back to him and in baggy jeans and the hood of their sweater covering their head Paddy couldn't even determine their gender, much less anything more specific. Without stopping to think he lunged at the attacker, diving head-first, spearing them around the waist. He floored the attacker, but they reacted quickly, twisting as they landed. Turning lithely, they shot out a firm hand; it pressed Paddy's face hard against the carpet. Springing forward, both their knees landed squarely on Paddy's back just below the shoulder blades, forcing the air out of his lungs in a rapid gasp. A wriggle, and their knees aligned up to his shoulders, either side of his head, securely pinning Paddy down; unable to move. He craned his face up off the floor, every ounce of strength fighting the hand forcing his head down, and briefly, just for a second, made eye contact with James Doyle. In the melee James had edged himself away, recoiling in a small crumpled ball in the corner of the room.

'Help me, please, your turn now,' Paddy's eyes implored. James looked directly at Paddy; his saviour pinned down by his hammer-wielding attacker. He knew the situation was desperate, he recognised the terror in Paddy's eyes, it matched his own. He gave a slow, silent, cautious nod and backing up hard against the wall began to rise, his arms spread wide for support and balance as he slid himself vertically upwards to a standing position. Paddy thrust and strained but his assailant had him trapped. Paddy grunted, his energy expended fruitlessly.

James Doyle, now standing, pressed himself tight into the corner as if he could spread across the wallpaper and camouflage himself out of harm's way. He understood Paddy's grunts were pleas for his aid and assistance, begging for him to return the favour and rid the danger. Paddy's eyes, by now the only thing he could move, flicked up and locked on to his again*: it's now or never, man*, they said. James Doyle nodded silently once more, and began peeling himself away from the wall. Ice-cold fear surged through his veins with an electric intensity, the hairs on his arms stood sentry-straight on raised bumps; a shiver made his jaw tremble. He took half a faltering step forward, his hands not yet leaving the walls, as if afraid he'd crumble if he'd let go. The ball of his foot made contact with the carpet: relief, he'd made it without disaster. He followed it with a wider, fuller step, and then another; his arms released from the wall and dropped to his side. Confidence trickled back within him; the tank no longer empty, it was out of the red warning zone and slowly started to rise. His fight, flight or freeze instincts reassessed the situation. Paddy watched; his eyes conveyed relief and thanks. James acknowledged them with a cold, guilty flick downwards, breaking the eye contact: *no no no, don't do it,* implored Paddy but James leapt to his left, darting for and through the open doorway. 'I'll call the police,' he yelled as if that was any consolation to the man on the floor with a hammer poised above his skull.

Paddy watched James Doyle's heels abandon him. Inside he collapsed, the fight in him extinguished. Any hope had gone, but that wasn't what lingered and filled his thoughts. Instead, Paddy was left with a sense of ironic justification: *I always said he was no good, I was right not to trust him, I always said there was something suspect about him, wait until I tell Monica I was right about him all along, she'll be sorry.*

The man above him readjusted his knees, and gripped Paddy tighter, his boots pressed in hard to Paddy's ribs. Paddy, to put it delicately, had been up close and personal with an impressive assortment of females in his time and never in his experience had they felt as hard and lumpy as this individual; combine that with the rasping noise to their breathing, and their sheer brutality so far, and Paddy was completely certain beyond any doubt that the person sitting on top of him was a man – but who? It seemed far too much of a coincidence that James, and then Paddy, happened to walk in on an opportunistic burglar so, as far as Paddy could see, there could only be one answer: Boot Camp Dan. If Paddy had worked out that James Doyle was the murderer then surely it stood to reason other people could have too? Paddy had lazily assumed all of Boot Camp Dan's fans were ladies of a certain age and disposition, much like the deranged Pamela who'd waged her vendetta against Monica, but murder was, of course, an equal opportunity employer and anyone of any age, gender or preference was welcome to take part.

'Listen,' Paddy said. He spoke with the loudest voice he could muster, his words muted against the face-full of carpet. His attacker sat directly across his back, depressing his ribcage; it made breathing difficult, and just speaking used what little air he had left in his lungs. He greedily snatched a half-breath and continued, trying to reason with the man on his back. 'Listen, I'm sorry about what happened to Boot Camp Dan. Honestly, I am, he didn't deserve that. But this won't make things right. I know you miss him—' An unexpected snort of derision erupted behind Paddy's ear. It confused him. 'I know you liked him.'

Another snort. The knees straddling Paddy loosened a little, affording him the chance to gulp down a lungful of air.

'I know his death caused you great upset and hurt—'

And another snort. The pressure on him eased again. The man had stopped channelling his entire weight through Paddy. There was also a change in the air: Paddy noticed that the man's breathing had lost its rasp, almost as if he was waiting for an audience to settle before speaking. Paddy took another deep breath, and released it; the man's grip around him didn't cling as it had before. A minute or so earlier his vice-like grip had restricted and controlled Paddy's movements; every breath he'd taken felt like fighting a straitjacket. Now, the grip had loosened, Paddy was certain of it. To be sure he drew another deep breath, stopping when he felt his ribs make contact with the man's boots. He exhaled, and when fully depleted estimated he had about an inch of tolerance all round; the man had become distracted by talk of Boot Camp Dan. Paddy realised he had a chance after all.

After a moment's thought that could change the entire course of his life, Paddy asked: 'Were you in love with him?'

He knew it was a gamble, and a risky one at that. He knew it could go only one of two ways: either it distracted the man even further and he would loosen his grip completely, or it totally disgusted him and in his rage he would slam his hammer down hard and fast behind Paddy's ear.

Monica and Paddy's grandmother had a romantic notion that gypsy blood flowed in their veins; an idea whispered to her when still a young girl no more than five or six by her own grandmother, on a long, sleepless night during an air raid. However, nobody gave it much credence. The word-of-mouth Minton history had since been so tidied, trimmed, pruned and prettified for middle-class acceptability the family tree now resembled a topiary hedge, but it was truer than any of them could've ever anticipated. Granny also claimed her distant Romany heritage blessed her with the gift of second sight: this however was an easier claim to disprove. At baby Monica's baptism, she'd declared with great certainty that when Leicester City won the League Monica would marry and have three beautiful babies of her own. Granny would often repeat this prophecy, usually at family events and gatherings, but Leicester City had languished without success for many years and looked set to languish for many more. But then, as Monica came of age and developed into an independent young woman Leicester City, who'd begun the season at odds of five thousand to one, went on an entirely unpredicted winning spree. At the Minton family Christmas dinner, traditionally the halfway point of the football season, Leicester City were still clinging to the top spot. Nobody watched Her Majesty's broadcast that year, Monica instead was the centre of attention: *have you got yourself a boyfriend, Monica; when are you going to introduce us; have you set a date yet?*

To the annoyance of Monica, and the amazement of everyone else in the country, Leicester City went on to win the League for the first and only time in its history. But, alas, there was no such historic win for Monica. Granny's gift was written off as nonsense, and she was relegated back to the role of family loon.

Nonetheless, Granny maintained she could correspond with the other realm and held firm in her assertion that her beloved Paddy had divine providence protecting him: *just before he came to join us here on Earth*, she'd say, *an angel kissed his lips and blessed him with good luck for his life ahead.*

So far, the blessing had stood him in good stead. Paddy had breezed through life on luck, charisma and charm without a single care in the world, and today it seemed was no different.

'Were you in love with him?'

Paddy's gamble had paid off, the angel's kiss held and luck favoured Paddy once more. The man sat back on his heels, resting. The shift in position raised his knees slightly, cantilevering the load off of Paddy's shoulders. The man scoffed again, and grumbles signified his disgust and contempt at such a suggestion. Although Paddy wasn't paying too much attention to his responses, he'd figured the man was no fan of Boot Camp Dan. But if he wasn't a vengeful fan, who was he?

The man cleared his throat, preparing to speak, but Paddy took his opportunity. Peeling his shoulders upwards towards the ceiling as far and as fast as he could muster caused the man to lose balance. Before he could right himself, Paddy pushed his knees down and forced his pelvis up. The man toppled over his head. Paddy scrabbled to his feet and started to run for the door without looking back.

The man on the ground lashed out, swinging his hammer wildly without aim or accuracy. It clipped Paddy's heel: not enough to cause injury, but enough to make him stumble. Paddy began to fall forwards and caught the edge of the desk to steady himself. He didn't turn, but knew from the sounds behind him that the man was on his feet and heading towards him. There, on the desk, right in front of him Paddy spotted a book: a diary or a notepad or something similar, the size of a novel about half an inch thick with a black leather cover and stiff sharp corners. He reached out and grabbed it.

AWARE OF THE MAN coming fast up behind him, Paddy spun around and hurled the book straight into his face, then dropped to the ground, hitting the carpet hard. The hammer ripped through the empty air where his head had been a half-second earlier.

Paddy dropped his shoulder and rolled out of harm's way. He reached the doorway and raced through, then covered the short distance in a leap to hurdle through the front entrance door left open by the cowardly Smoothie in his earlier run for safety. He cleared the door; the evening breeze chilled the sheen of sweat on his face, electrifying his senses. He heard the running fast-paced footsteps behind him and the rasp of the man's heavy breathing; no time to slow and look behind himself, he knew his priority was to open up some distance if he was to be safe.

'Paddy, get down,' a voice to his side called out. Instinct, reflex and fear commandeered his motor controls without thought getting in the way, and in total obedience he flung himself to the ground, slapping hard on to the cool damp grass.

Behind him he heard a swish, slicing through the air, going straight into a hard solid strike. Then a groan cried out, followed by a slow collapse.

Paddy rolled out to his back. The endless indigo starless sky above brought him a sense of serenity; his breathing slowed to normal and the drumming of his heartbeat faded from his ears. Monica, of all people, hove into his view. She offered a hand and helped him to his feet. He turned back, to see the house, to understand what had just happened and was astonished by the sight: the crumpled heap of his attacker lay face down, unmoving, on the path, his face still covered by his hoodie, and beside him DC Nicci Sharma was still brandishing her police-issue extendable baton.

The two women looked at Paddy, then each other, and smiled. They'd solved the case and stopped a killer from killing again. They'd done it.

CHAPTER **TWENTY FIVE**

'RIGHT, SO RUN ME through that again. Everything,' Nicci Sharma said to Monica, but didn't take her eyes from the road. She punished the small engine of her hatchback; it whined at the harsh demands, and made painful crunches at jerky, snatched gear changes. At its nose, the concealed blue siren lights flashed their urgency. The traffic ahead parted and they tore along the suburban streets at a frightening speed.

Monica pushed herself back in her seat, one hand gripping the door handle, the other firmly planted on the dashboard: always a nervous passenger, this was like the worst roller coaster imaginable. In her terror she could barely think, much less put forward a compelling case. She became aware of Nicci Sharma staring at her with an expectant look: *watch the road, watch the road* pleaded Monica; if only she could get the words out.

Monica took a deep breath, and closed her eyes to settle her thoughts: if she answered Nicci Sharma then perhaps she'd turn her attention back to the road. Monica re-opened her eyes and sought a fixed point in the far distance to anchor herself; all the jostling and rolling made her seasick. She gave a long exhale, then began to explain at a machine-gun break-neck speed.

'Paddy and I, we were at James Doyle's house to feed his cat. I found his file about Boot Camp Dan. I wasn't prying, honestly, it was ... just there. Anyway, I took a quick look. James had sunk a lot of money in to Boot Camp Dan. He'd spent a fortune on stylists, on websites and advertising, on ghostwriters to do all his social media for him, loads, it was an absolute fortune. Anyway, he found out a few weeks ago that Boot Camp Dan was disgraced, that he was a drug cheat. I guess he thought he could brazen it out, say he'd done his time and was a reformed character, everyone deserves a second chance and all of that. However, he hadn't anticipated Herr Geerhart.'

'Hair ...?'

'Herr Geerhart. He's an investor, from Geneva, proper mega-money. Comes from an old Swiss banking family and he's about a thousand years old. James Doyle has a network of various investors, several were at the launch event, but Geerhart is the principal one and he's the weather vane.'

'Weather ...?'

'Weather vane. The others look at him to decide what they should do. If Geerhart likes something, they all want to be a part of it. If he doesn't, they all avoid it.'

'And this Geerhart, where's he fit into it then?'

'Geerhart had got his own people to do their own due diligence, instead of just relying on the investors' prospectus created by James Doyle. Geerhart discovered for himself about Boot Camp Dan's drug cheat history.'

'And he wasn't impressed with James Doyle's deception?'

'I don't know if you'd call it deception as such—'

'Had he told him about it?'

'No—'

'Then I call it deception.'

'Fair enough. But it ran deeper than that. From what I gather, Herr Geerhart comes from a deeply traditional Christian upbringing and on top of that he has a personal passion for only investing in ethical and sustainable schemes.'

'And?'

'I found a letter in the file from his lawyer. It said that from what their due diligence uncovered about Boot Camp Dan, it was unable to reconcile it against Herr Geerhart's commitment to ethical family values and so he was withdrawing from the venture with immediate effect.'

'And when was that letter sent?'

'No idea, but it was received the same day of Boot Camp Dan's murder. Paddy and I met James's postman, he told us he does his rounds about eight every morning so—'

'So James Doyle would've received it a few hours before Boot Camp Dan was murdered?'

'Exactly. Now, think about it: if James worked on the assumption that nobody yet knew about Geerhart's withdrawal, he could've pushed ahead with the live launch event that same morning and tried to blag his way with the investors present that all was hunky-dory and get them to sign on the dotted line before news of Geerhart became public knowledge.'

'Or?'

'Or he reads the letter, admits defeat and sees the deal as dead in the water and he faces financial ruin; as I say his costs were colossal.'

'Fine. I can see either side of that. But what's Paddy got into his head?'

'Insurance.'

'Insurance?'

'In either of those scenarios I've just described, if the deal collapses because he can't sell it, that's just bad luck, that's his own commercial risk to bear. However, if it collapses because of an unforeseen incident that makes it impossible to complete the deal, he can claim against the insurance policy we discovered in his file.'

'And Boot Camp Dan—'

'He was the deal. The whole concept of the deal was Boot Camp Dan, without him there's nothing. So, either he'd heard news of Geerhart's decision had reached the other investors, or he'd made his mind up before he got to the park, but with Boot Camp Dan dead he can recover all his costs through the insurance.'

Nicci Sharma spent a few moments examining the notion from all sides before speaking again. 'I suppose it does sound like a pretty solid motive, if he thinks it would rescue him from financial ruin. And I'm no psychologist, but I'd imagine his opinion towards Boot Camp Dan changed quite substantially, and not in a good way, which may have made it easier for him to justify it to himself.'

'And don't forget he was the only one other than Boot Camp Dan who could come and go through that backstage curtain without anyone thinking anything of it, like when everyone else was busy getting ready for the re-launch.'

'Very true, that does sound like a compelling case for motive and opportunity. And that's what Paddy's going to confront him with?'

'Yes,' replied Monica. 'He'll be okay, won't he?'

'Paddy is probably the most charming person I've ever met, he could sweet-talk anyone, but then if James Doyle has already killed, well, that changes a person—'

Neither woman spoke after that, there was no need, they knew the answer to the question but almost as if in silent response, Nicci pushed the car even harder.

'UP HERE, ON THE RIGHT,' directed Monica. She pointed to a narrow turning; the approach to James Doyle's gated enclave. It had no signposting which was exactly how the residents liked it, discreetly hidden from the leafy public highway.

'I must've driven this street thousands of times over the years,' said Nicci, 'but I've never spotted this turning before.' The narrow approach resembled more a wide driveway, travelling up between two newish detached houses in the similar faux-historic style as James Doyle's place; Monica had noticed it on her first visit and presumed they were by the same developer. A short distance past the houses they came upon the iron gates, firmly closed shut. Whirring down her window, Nicci Sharma began jabbing every button on the kerbside voice-box with much impatience: *come on, come on*.

Monica shook her by the arm: 'Look, it's him!'

Facing them through the iron railings of the gate was the face of Handsome Smoothie, James Doyle; except, he didn't look that Handsome. The way he gripped hold of the bars and the terrified expression on his face, he looked like he was in maximum security lock-up.

Monica was aware of movement to her side; Nicci retrieved her extendable baton from the side pocket of the door, and wrapped its loop around her wrist. She caught Monica looking at it. 'Just in case he starts anything.'

With a clank the gates began to roll open by themselves, some amenable neighbour pressing the button in response to Nicci's earlier requests.

James took a step back, then hurtled towards their car as fast as he could, sprinting the short distance. Nicci's fingers flexed around the baton; her grip tightened as her reflexes sharpened, ready for danger. James came close to the car, his hand snatching at the door handles.

Nicci brought her elbow up to her chest, her fist clenched the baton at shoulder level, braced and ready to bring it down to defend herself the moment James breached the car. The back door behind Nicci's position in the driving seat opened, James clambered in, Nicci turned, poised to strike him down.

'Thank God you're here,' his voice a whimpering pant. 'Bless you. You've saved my life.' Then, as an afterthought he remembered, 'Paddy! He's got Paddy. We need to save Paddy.'

Nicci slammed the car into gear. It lurched away noisily from a standing start, and sped the length of the quiet, residential cul-de-sac with all the savagery of a Grand Prix circuit. Monica turned in her seat to get a good look at James, his face and shirt smothered in dried blood, his eye swollen and almost closed, his clothes damaged and torn.

'James,' Monica spoke in tones she thought sympathetic and soothing, 'how about you tell us exactly what's been going on?'

And so, he did.

REQUESTING ARMED BACK-UP, Nicci snapped off the radio and got out of the car. She'd pulled up alongside the kerb, outside James's house. Grabbing her baton, she threw open her door and got out of the car; flicking her wrist as soon as she was outside, the baton extended to its full length.

Sounds emanated from the house; angry, destructive sounds and animalistic grunts. Nicci Sharma stood still on the footpath approaching the house and took stock of the situation. With a downward swat of the hand she gestured for Monica and James to stay back behind the car, out of harm's way. Gripping her baton in her right hand she raised it up past her left shoulder, ready to bring it down in a hard, fast backhand swing; she took a cautious step forwards.

A figure burst through the open doorway. The surprise gave a cold beat in her chest. Another figure followed through. In a nanosecond she needed to process the scene and act accordingly; she instantly recognised the first figure as Paddy, in a state of panic. Behind him came a figure in a hoodie sweater but she was very definite: he was in pursuit of Paddy, not fleeing with him.

'Paddy, get down!'

Paddy dropped, throwing himself flat against the grass. Nicci swung her hardest; the baton scythed through the air catching the pursuer squarely on the side of the neck. The force of the blow lifted the pursuer off their feet, their momentum tipping them over on to their side. They fell to the ground with the same delicacy as a sack of potatoes. Groaning, their shoulder made impact with the pavement first, then they rolled and lay face down where they didn't move. Nicci Sharma stood over them, baton drawn just in case they leapt up in a surprise attack. To the edge of her vision, she could see Monica helping Paddy to his feet.

Paddy stared at the crumpled heap on the pavement, then back towards James Doyle who'd lingered out of harm's way beside the car: 'I was convinced it was him,

Mon. Absolutely convinced, but then when I got here and found … this.' Paddy wafted a loose arm in no particular direction, but Monica understood what he meant.

PRODDING THE BODY on the ground with her toe, Monica gave loud, clear instructions to it: 'You can get up now.'

There was no response. She prodded again. Harder this time: 'I said, you can get up now, Tim.'

Refusing to believe his ears, and refusing to be patient, Paddy crouched, grabbed his assailant's shoulders and hauled him up off the floor. Yanking down the hood, he looked straight into the eyes of Comedy Tim.

Paddy couldn't reconcile what he was seeing, 'But … what—'

Monica took Paddy's hand. As she turned them away and began to lead Paddy back to the safe haven of the car, Nicci Sharma formally placed Comedy Tim under arrest, and handcuffed him.

'I don't understand, Monica,' he began but couldn't find the words to carry on. Monica, however, knew exactly what he needed to hear, having been advised only minutes earlier by the Handsome Smoothie.

'You were halfway right, Paddy,' she offered. 'It did all come down to the insurance. It's just the wrong person.'

'I can see that, Mon, but … what?'

'Remember when we looked through the file we found in James's office?'

'You looked through.'

'Whatever. Anyway, remember me saying James had sunk an absolute fortune into developing Boot Camp Dan as a brand? All the designers, stylists, clothing, websites and advertising and so on?' Paddy nodded, hoping this was all leading somewhere he could understand. 'If you remember, one big cost was a ghostwriter to write all his social media? Someone to monitor the accounts and write funny little quips and comments, make jokes and stuff?'

Paddy nodded again, but this time a picture was beginning to emerge. 'That was Tim?'

Monica grinned: *by Jove, he's got it!*

'That was Tim,' she confirmed. 'I thought it was odd; every time I ever met him he had a screen in front of him, always texting or posting stuff. Now of course it makes sense, it was his job.'

'But, if it was his job—'

Monica cut him off, knowing exactly what he was going to ask. 'He never got paid. Boot Camp Dan never paid anyone anything. He'd ask for more and more, and if anyone queried the cost he'd either fob them off saying it was good exposure or he'd pass them back to James to deal with. James, however, couldn't afford to pay all the bills Dan was racking up. James was relying on getting the investors on board, having them sign up, and then he'd be able to clear all the debts he and Boot Camp Dan had accrued.'

'Sounds like a bit of an over-the-top reaction though, Mon' replied Paddy, 'for just a few tweets and posts?'

'Not according to James Doyle.' Something chimed in the back of Monica's memory. 'And not according to Hazel either.'

'Hazel?'

'Remember the talk about Comedy Tim's big audition recently?' she replied. Paddy dimly recalled it being discussed around the table at the Munsters'. 'The suggestion from Hazel was the audition didn't go very well, and he blamed Boot Camp Dan.'

'Boot Camp Dan was a thief,' shouted a voice behind them. They turned in surprise to find Tim there, controlled and steered at the elbow by Nicci Sharma. 'I'd been working towards that audition for years. They call it the Hit Factory on the circuit because of the number of big-name stars it churns out, and it was my turn, I'd earned it. I go in, I give them all of my best stuff and not a laugh, not even a smile. And when done, the producer says to me: you need to write your own material, you can't come here with someone else's lines. They accused me of plagiarism – to my face!'

Paddy glanced across to Monica, she glanced back, neither seeming to know how to respond but luckily for them Comedy Tim hadn't finished.

'This producer, he said that he knew all my jokes as he'd heard them all before, that I'd robbed them from Boot Camp Dan. I was livid. I'd been writing stuff for him, but I didn't know he'd been copying down all my best gags as well, nicking my greatest hits. They'd seen Boot Camp Dan do them and thought I'd stolen from him, not the other way around.'

'And you killed him for that?' asked Paddy.

'I was fuming at him. Then on the day of the big live launch event, you went and ruined the opening for him.' Tim looked straight at Monica; the burn of embarrassment flared beneath her eyes just at the thought of that morning. 'And then I get a call from him, demanding I come and see him. So I go over to find him, leaving you lot at the Munsters, and there he is behind his pathetic little curtain thinking he's Mr Hollywood at the Oscars or something and he tells me he needs a red-hot opening line, something hilarious and brilliant to use when they restart the live launch that'll cover up the beginning you botched up.'

'Yes, alright, you don't need to keep on about it,' snapped Monica: *confession's all very good for the soul, but stop bringing me in to it.*

'So, I asked him: what's in it for me? He asked: what do you mean? And I told him about the audition. I said I wanted him to join me in a phone call to that producer to explain I was his writer and to give me the credit I deserved.'

'And I'm guessing he said no?'

'He said more than that. He said I was nobody and that I would always be a nobody whereas he was going to be a star. He said he would've taken me with him as his writer but not now, that I was fired. He said there was no point bleating about it as no-one would believe me as he was Boot Camp Dan and I was no-one.'

'And then?'

'Then, with nothing to lose and nothing to gain, I demanded my money. I said I wanted paying for everything I'd done for him. He refused and again told me I was worthless and that as it had all been posted in his name, it all belonged to him. I was so angry. I was furious with him. But then ...'

'Yes?' asked Monica and Paddy in unison.

'He told me to get lost, that he needed to prepare for his big entrance. You know what he was like, all about the high energy. Next thing I know he's on all fours doing push-ups to get the adrenalin pumping. I'm seeing red, I'm so angry and there's a set of dumbbells right there, next to me. He looks up, gives me, "Are you still here, loser? Get out before I call security," then looks down again. Before I know what I've done I've smacked a dumbbell across the back of his head, he looks at me all groggy and I realise if he tells anyone then I'm in serious trouble. I know I need to finish him off and I give him another whack but I can't pull it out, it's got wedged in too deep but he's not moving. And so, I ran. And that was that.'

'Hold on,' Paddy protested, 'you can't say that's that. What was today all about?'

'Well,' Comedy Tim sucked the side of his cheek, looking for the right words, 'that's your fault, Paddy. If the first incident was down to Monica, today was down to you.'

'And how do you work that out?'

'Because you were the one shouting off about insurance policies, remember? You're the one who told us that James Doyle was claiming against an insurance policy that would pay him out all the costs he'd incurred for Boot Camp Dan, and you were the one telling us he'd allowed in his accounts for a writer: that's me. Whether or not he'd actually paid me, those were my costs. So, with Boot Camp Dan dead, and my comedy career with it, I at least should be able to walk away with the money I'd earnt. Surely that's fair, isn't it?

Paddy had to admit, in a strange sort of way it was.

'When I heard James Doyle was due back today, I decided I'd come and see him. I told him I wanted paying. He said he had no money to pay me, and he'd written Boot Camp Dan off as a bad loss and was moving on and I should do the same. I said that simply wouldn't do, and I wasn't leaving until I got my money. Things got heated, and quickly overboiled ... and that's when you walked in.'

'I see.'

'So, now you're all done and up to date.'

CHAPTER **TWENTY SIX**

'SO YOU'RE ALL DONE and up to date,' said Paddy to the astonished, open-mouthed faces circled around him. Even Mr Munster looked on in astonished interest. Hazel was the first to break the silence.

'Well I never. Who'd have thought it? A killer in our midst.'

'I bet your research never showed that, did it?' replied Pete, enjoying getting a little dig in at Hazel.

'You know what, the first thing I'm going to do when I get home is dig out my file on Tim.'

Glances with raised eyebrows over scuttled around the gathering: *file?* they all queried without saying it aloud.

Hazel didn't notice, and blathered on regardless. 'I'll squirrel up and down his family tree, see if I can spot any wrong 'uns that might've given us a clue as to how he'd turn out.'

'You can't blame the ancestors,' replied Kenton, 'sins of the father and all that. No, I think the poor chap was provoked too far and finally snapped. It's all about circumstances. It's nothing to do with your family, look at these two.' A big square hand wafted in the direction of Paddy and Monica. 'They're family, but you couldn't tell.'

'How so?' demanded Paddy, feeling defensive and offended both at the same time and not understanding why.

'I guess you've got a point,' conceded Hazel.

'Has he?' Paddy still didn't understand if he was being criticised or pitied.

'Yeah, I can see that too,' chipped in Pete.

'Do you know what they're on about, Monica?' asked the frantic Paddy.

Monica ruminated for a moment and watched a seagull take a slow glide out over the river. She popped the lid off her paper cup and raised it to her lips, taking a tentative sip, 'Mmm, tastes flowery, must be mine. I think what they're trying to say, Paddy, is that you're the easy-going free spirit you've always been, and me, I'm the serious corporate business woman.'

Around the table heads nodded.

Paddy paused, letting the words sink in for a moment, then raised a question that had been on his mind: 'About that Monica, it's been a peculiar couple of weeks. Is the corporate rat race tempting you back?'

'No,' replied Monica, 'I work for *We Sit Pets*, in fact I'm the only professional dogwalker here.'

THE END

ABOUT THE **AUTHOR**

Matthew Ross was born and raised in the Medway Towns, England. He still lives in Kent with his Kiwi wife, his children and a very bouncy dog.

He was immersed in the building industry from a very early age helping out on his father's sites during school holidays before launching into his own career at 17. He's worked on projects ranging from the smallest domestic repair to £billion+ infrastructure, and probably everything in between.

A lifelong comedy nerd, he ticked off a bucket-list ambition and tried his hand at stand-up comedy. Whilst being an experience probably best forgotten (for both him and audiences alike) it ignited a love for writing, leading to various commissions including for material broadcast on BBC Radio 4 comedy shows.

Matthew moved into the longer format of novel writing after graduating from the Faber Academy in London in 2017.

Matthew enjoys reading all manner of books – especially crime and mystery; 80s music; and travelling and can't wait for the next trip to New Zealand to spend time with family and friends.

ACKNOWLEDGEMENTS

It may well be the case that it was the amazing cover that made you pick this book up, and that is thanks entirely to Patrick Knowles leading the design process with verve and passion.

I owe a big thank you to Abbie Headon for the structural and editorial support – and for correcting my appalling punctuation.

Of course, I must thank my family. Thank you to my wife Rebecca, who put up with me lost in my own little word for hours on end whilst I worked on this. Thank you to my two boys who inspired me that it's never too late to follow a dream.

And finally, thank you for taking the time and trouble to read this book, it's more appreciated than you may ever realise. If you enjoyed it please do leave a review, your feedback would be great.

I'd love to hear from you so please do feel free to get in touch with me. You can find me by the methods below:

matthew@mattwross.uk

@mattwross

@mattw_ross

www.mattwross.uk

Printed in Great Britain
by Amazon

33476772R00159